T0049242

Tales
Abstracted

Tales Abstracted

Edmund R. Malinowski

authorHOUSE®

AuthorHouse™
1663 Liberty Drive
Bloomington, IN 47403
www.authorhouse.com
Phone: 1-800-839-8640

© 2012 by Edmund R. Malinowski. All rights reserved.

No part of this book may be reproduced, stored in a retrieval system, or transmitted by any means without the written permission of the author.

Published by AuthorHouse   09/29/2012

ISBN: 978-1-4772-6893-3 (sc)
ISBN: 978-1-4772-6895-7 (e)

Library of Congress Control Number: 2012916748

Any people depicted in stock imagery provided by Thinkstock are models, and such images are being used for illustrative purposes only.
Certain stock imagery © Thinkstock.

This book is printed on acid-free paper.

Because of the dynamic nature of the Internet, any web addresses or links contained in this book may have changed since publication and may no longer be valid. The views expressed in this work are solely those of the author and do not necessarily reflect the views of the publisher, and the publisher hereby disclaims any responsibility for them.

Acknowledgments

After my mother bought me a typewriter I started writing these tales as a teenager in 1948. Upon reading a few tales my brothers, Richard and John, were so excited that they were quickly inspired to contribute several surprise-ending stories. Fifty of these short short stories were compiled into volume one.

Some 29 years later, volume one was discovered by my youngest son, Robert, who, as a teenager, contributed several original tales, which, in 1993, were compiled into volume two consisting of 50 short short stories.

In 2012 the stories in these two volumes were edited and combined into the current book containing 10 Doses (chapters), each Dose containing 10 stories.

Dedication

This book is dedicated to my mother, Stella, who inspired me to write.

Tales Abstracted

*T*hese tales are written for those who love to read short stories, very short stories, that excite the senses.

They are written for those who are fascinated by the abstractions of life, life outside as well as inside this world. They will take you to worlds you have never seen before, will probably never see again and may never want to see again. They are miniature versions of the Twilight Zone and Outer Limits.

Each abstracted tale is limited to two pages and is designed to grasp your full attention from the first sentence to the very last sentence which often contains an unexpected twist.

These tales will feed your cravings for spine-tingling ghost stories, space adventure, heart-beating love stories, science fiction, philosophy, nightmares, nonsense, insanity, sanity, absurdity, the macabre, the bizarre, humor, pathos, and all the other sensations imaginable.

Tales Abstracted will play tricks on your imagination. They are guaranteed to take your breath away and shock you into reality.

Those who do not possess an abstract mind are warned to refrain from casting their eyes upon any page of this book, lest a great evil dispel upon them.

The author assumes no liability for damages or consequences, direct or indirect, resulting from the reading or retelling of these tales.

May be habit forming.

Parental guidance recommended.

Pleasant dreams.

Contents

Third Dose

Fourth Dose

Fifth Dose

Sixth Dose

Seventh Dose

Eight Dose

Ninth Dose

Tenth Dose

First Dose

I'm Not Me

*T*hat man is me!

How can that be?

I know who I am. And I'm not me . . . That man, over there, sitting on the bench, looking this way with the smile on his face, that's me!

Are you sure?

He's me. I'm him. Don't you understand?

You're positive?

He's me. He's in my body. I'm in his body. He's me. I'm him. It's as simple as that. I'm not me. I'm him. He's me . . . For heaven's sake, why can't someone understand?

Calm down. Don't get overly excited. Tell me more. Start from the beginning . . . Sit down. I insist . . . Now tell me everything you know, from the beginning.

I don't know what happened . . . This morning I woke up as usual . . . had breakfast . . . and went for my usual morning stroll through the park. A funny-looking man, with a large proboscis and a handle-bar mustache, walked towards me. I took particular notice of him because he strutted peculiarly . . . When we were about two or three feet away from each other, he turned his head in my direction and I thought he was going to speak . . .

. . . Yes, then what happened?

I really don't know . . . Just as his lips began to move . . . I felt a blinding flash . . . and was engulfed by a dizziness that I never experienced before . . . Then . . . Then . . .

Yes, go on. Then what happened?

Then, when the whirling in my head subsided . . . I suddenly realized . . . that I was walking in the opposite direction . . . At first I thought I must have spun around during the dizzy spell . . . I was startled to see myself, clothes and all, walking past myself . . . I felt a strangeness inside . . . something was different . . . My fingers were fatter. My hands were larger. My clothes were different . . . Somehow that strange man and I had changed places . . .

I thought so . . . You have just confirmed my suspicions . . . Something strange has indeed inflicted our world . . .

What makes you say that?

You see, my dear confused man, you are occupying my body.

A Penny for
Your Thought

"*A* penny for your thought," he said.

And the next thing I knew was . . . that somehow . . . I had lost a thought . . . I mean that, somehow or other, my mind seemed to skip a beat . . . Somehow, my mind went blank . . . absolutely blank . . . blank for just a fleeting second . . . And I don't remember what I was thinking about . . .

And then I was back to thinking again.

I was thinking about something or someone when suddenly this queer little man pops up out of nowhere and says, "A penny for your thought." The next thing I knew . . . I forgot what I was thinking . . . And here, in my right hand, was a penny.

And, for all the life of me, I *still* cannot remember what it was I was thinking about.

It's weird, like one of those strange things that happen in your life that somehow you cannot explain.

Anyhow, I thought I should tell you . . . for the record . . . in case it should happen to you . . . or someone else.

Of course, I've done a lot of thinking since this happened. I honestly believe that we have been secretly visited by people from another world or, perhaps, another dimension. These creatures need our thoughts. Being that they are honest citizens of their own world they are equally honest with us. They pay us for our thoughts . . . A penny a thought . . . Fair enough . . .

To them thoughts are food. They digest these thoughts like you and I eat and drink. It nourishes their functional cells. They store them like we store electricity in batteries.

You see, thoughts are electrical impulses. These creatures feed on electrical impulses. Without such impulses they cannot exist.

How delicious our strange, barbaric thoughts must appear to them.

Yet I cannot help thinking that these people sell and trade them to one another . . . And, most importantly, they . . .

Now what's this? Another penny?

Now where was I?

Can't remember what I was going to say.

It was important . . . It was most important . . .

It was the real solution to the mystery . . .

I know it was.

Let me think . . . What was I going to tell you?

The Martians
Are Here

$\mathcal{T}$he spaceship raced across the sky with atomic precision. The rocky planet of Mars was overpopulated. To seek new fertile land was necessary for survival.

Onion spoke: Earth is a likely place to settle. The test probe indicates that the atmosphere and climate are similar to our home planet of Mars.

Carrot agreed: Very similar indeed. I say we land there.

Apple was cynical: I don't like those clouds. I say we move on to a more promising land.

Cabbage interjected: But our fuel is low.

Celery said: We have not been able to test the soil since our soil-tester probe smashed on Venus. We must be careful. Landing is very risky.

Watermelon bellowed: Let's land and test the soil ourselves. At least temporarily. If it is inhabitable we can always move on again.

Oak added: Perhaps we can find some fuel on Earth. Our fuel is critically low.

Apple cautioned: I don't like those clouds. They're too thick.

Onion spoke: We should land while we still have some fuel. Else we will soon be stranded in outer space.

Tobacco quipped: Move on . . . Move on . . .

Celery yawned: Stop here.

The ship, filled with quarreling Martians, moved straight on course passing tantalizingly close to the Earth.

Apple suggested a vote and they all agreed. The vote was overwhelmingly unanimous.

The space ship landed safely on Earth on a huge mountain of rock. The land was beautiful. Clean, clear and warm with sunshine. The rocky terrain resembled Mars. How surprising.

Carrot suggested they settle in the valley below. The thousands of Martians moved down the rocky mountain with enthusiasm. But the clouds above quickly darkened.

The rain fell freely and mercilessly. And the Martians were quickly swept down to the valley into a bed of soft, soggy dirt.

They sank into the soil becoming rooted to the ground, sprouting hideous limbs in the oddest places, above and below. They were transformed into monstrosities. They were trapped by the Earth . . . And they cried and cursed this demon planet.

Subconscious Inversion

"Watch this carefully," whispered Dr. Gastone as he limped, ape-like, across the room to the control panel. "Watch closely," he reiterated. Then he pulled the switch.

Dr. Crawley bit the tip of his lip, in contemplation. "Well?" he asked sarcastically. "I see nothing unusual."

Dr. Gastone bounced across the room to the experimental table. Inside the wire-meshed cage lay a small cat, stunned by the electricity. He shook the cage until the cat awoke. It snarled like a tiger and clawed fiercely at the doctor who was amply protected by the cage. It tore and chewed the wire mesh, hissed and spat.

"See," said Gastone, "One minute ago the cat was gentle. Now it is a wild animal."

Dr. Crawley scratched his stubby beard. "Explain your theory again, doctor," he urged.

"It's very simple. A subject placed in a crossed magnetic field, when given a jolt of an electric field of the proper frequency at the critical angle, will undergo subconscious inversion."

"What do you mean, subconscious inversion?"

"The subconscious mind becomes the conscious mind, and the conscious mind becomes the subconscious mind. You see, the cat is now living in its subconscious state. Its subconscious mind has taken full control of its conscious state. Its true inner self is in full control of its outer state."

"A very nice theory, Dr. Gastone, but I must beg to differ. The cat was merely provoked by the sudden shock of electricity. Nothing more."

"No! No! It's true, I tell you. The cat is functioning by its subconscious mind. It is controlled by its latent instincts . . . Let me perform one more experiment to prove my theory correct," begged Dr. Gastone. "Please remove the cat. Wear these gloves."

Just when Dr. Crawley reached inside the cage to remove the cat, Dr. Gastone pulled the switch again. A jolt of electricity flashed through the cage, passing through the gloves.

"Now, what do you think of my theory?"

"It's true," replied Dr. Crawley, his hair cascading wildly, a sinister smile forming on his lips. "Everything you said is true. This is an amazing discovery. The subconscious mind does take control of the body . . . Too bad you will not live long enough to get credit for your discovery."

The Magic Rosin

Agaldini smashed his fist against the piano, shook his violin and wept bitterly. The maestro rose from the piano and patted miserable Agaldini on the back to console him. But Agaldini brushed him away rudely.

"I don't need your sympathy," he growled. "The music does not flow from my violin the way I want it to."

The maestro soothed him cautiously. "My son, you play well but you lack spark and confidence. All great virtuosos have a spark of the supernatural . . . And I believe I know how to give you that supernatural spark . . . Trust me . . ." With that, the maestro left the sobbing Agaldini to himself.

Moments later he returned carrying a soft, black, felt bag with a golden chain. "Here," he said smilingly, "put this on your bow . . . It is magic rosin . . . There is no more . . . It is five hundred years old . . . I have been saving it for someone like you . . . Believe me, with this magic rosin on your bow your violin will play more powerfully and more majestically than any violin in the world."

Agaldini looked hard at the small bag. His eyes glowed with excitement and anticipation. He sensed the power of the magic rosin immediately.

His heart beat in rhythm as he gingerly rubbed the bow across the rosin. His senses were greeted by a mystical fragrance that emanated from the rosin. The bow seemed to pulsate in his hands . . . Truly, this was magic rosin . . .

The maestro played a piano introduction and paused briefly for the violin to begin. Agaldini inhaled, then pulled his bow firmly across the strings. A clear, rich, vibrating tone filled the room. It was indeed magic. He played on and on and on. Each note was perfect in pitch. Each note carried its own beauty, yet melted into the next note. The bow seemed alive. It danced on the strings. It moved effortlessly. It seemed to play by itself.

Agaldini became rich and famous. The world enjoyed his virtuosity.

But soon the rosin was worn to nearly nothing, and young Agaldini became worried.

"Maestro," he begged, "you must find me more magic rosin."

"My son," the maestro replied, "there never was any magic rosin. That was your own old rosin . . . I simply put it in a fancy bag."

The Beat

Listen.

Thump . . . Thump . . . Thump . . .

Do you hear the beat?"

Thump . . . Thump . . . Thump . . .

There it is again.

Thump . . . Thump . . . Thump . . .

Yes, yes, there it is . . . I hear it. Loud and clear . . . You must hear it . . . There it beats again.

Thump . . . Thump . . . Thump . . .

Are you deaf? The beats are loud and clear, . . . rhythmic.

Thump . . . Thump . . . Thump . . .

Good heavens, my whole body is vibrating with staccato beat. My mind is delirious with joy, the joy of living and breathing. I can feel energy soaring through my veins, beating through my arteries. It is exhilarating."

Thump . . . Thump . . . Thump . . .

How beautiful is the sound. You must hear it. The vibrations echo through my body. On and on it beats.

Repeating itself in regular, monotonous, pounding beats. Like a symphony of life. Completely captivating.

Thump . . . Thump . . . Thump . . .

Can't you feel it? . . . No? . . . You must have lost your senses. It is loud and clear.

Thump . . . Thump . . . Thump . . .

Can't you feel it? . . . It is like a jack-hammer pounding away . . ."

Thump . . . Thump . . . Thump . . .

Listen closely.

Thump . . . Thump . . . Thump . . .

Closer . . . Look closer . . . Listen closer . . . Open your ears . . . Are you deaf? . . . What is wrong with you? . . . Listen . . . Listen! . . .

Thump . . . Thump . . . Thump . . .

There it goes again. You do hear it? . . . Listen carefully . . . You must hear it! . . . The beating is there . . .

Thump . . . Thump . . . .

You do hear it! . . . Come back! . . . Come back!

Thump . . . .

Come back, doctor! . . . I can hear the beating. Surely, you can hear the beating . . . Come back, doctor! I am not dead . . . Listen . . .

A Time for Humor

Can you imagine a perfect stranger coming up to you, tapping you on the shoulder and saying, "I'm from the future. I've come to visit the past."?

That's exactly what happened to Elroy Shultz.

But Elroy had a good sense of humor and went along with the gag. "That's odd," he said, "so am I."

The meek, little stranger was startled. "What a coincidence. What year are you from?"

Elroy decided to play along with the joke. "I'm from the Psychoamniastic Period . . . the year 23645 AD."

The stranger scratched his head and said meekly, "That *is* long after my time. I'm from the year 5956 AD. My name is Gruzzelfurk." He extended his arm and they shook hands like old friends.

"My name is Elroy Shultzingleberganderlostleranderson."

The stranger smiled and with perfect pronunciation responded, "I'm very pleased to make your acquaintance

Mr. Elroy Shultzingleberganderlostleranderson." Elroy was amazed by his excellent diction . . . and memory.

"Tell me, what year is it at the present time?" the stranger asked.

"2993," Elroy fibbed. The year was, in truth, 1993.

"Heavens forbid," cried the strange little man, "I've miscalculated. I'm off course by one thousand years. I'll never get back . . . Do you know anything about Inner-dimensional Analysis of Time Stress?"

Elroy smiled. "My lord, Mr. Gruzeff(?), how far behind the times you are. Inner-d went out with the stone age. Haven't you heard about the Systematic Depopulable Energistic Time Transformation?"

The little man was extremely worried. "Heavens no. That must be way after my time. You must help me get back to my initial time period." A hint of hysteria choked his high pitched voice.

"I will be very glad to help," Elroy replied. Barely able to hold back his laughter, he opened the doors of the telephone booth and said with deliberate seriousness, "Please, step inside this time capsule."

Tears formed in the stranger's eyes. "Thank you," he said.

"Your welcome," Elroy replied, as he walked away smiling.

A Visit to Earth

The spaceship landed on the barren desert at the spot designated by the Earth council. Out of the saucer-like sphere emerged the first Martians, their green tentacles groping deeply and inquisitively into the hot sand.

The Earth reception committee stepped forward, gesturing in order to make some form of contact with these unusual visitors. The Martians stared amusingly, then one of them began to speak.

"Fear not, Third Planetarians, for we have come on a mission of peace, not war. I speak your language fluently because our scientists have discovered a process of emulating any form of vocal or telepathic communication by determining the subliminal capacity of brain waves being emitted. This should not surprise you since you are well aware of our mastery of space flight."

The Earth Representative stepped forward. "We of planet Earth welcome you as our friends from outer space. Please tour our planet as you wish."

The Martians were shocked to see the land. "Why is your land so devastated?" they asked.

The Earthling spoke, "It is the result of the Great War, a war that almost completely destroyed the entire Earth."

"But why was there such a war?"

". . . Because of hate, anger, distrust, lust for power, and greed for wealth."

"Who could have been so self-seeking?"

"Two races once existed on this Earth, each believing itself to be superior to the other. A conflict over possession of a small island in the Pacific Ocean lead to sporadic fighting. This conflict grew out of proportion, precipitating a nuclear holocaust that destroyed every city in the world . . ."

"What is that creature, over there, drooling on the ground?"

"He is a member of the super-race that started the Great War. He and all others of his kind are suffering from radiation poisoning and will soon die as helpless maniacs.

"It is so unfortunate . . . And now we must return to our home planet with our report of the Earth . . . But we will return soon."

The Martian and the Earthling rubbed tentacles as they both said in unison, "Good-bye, brother Ant."

Who Speaks?

"**A**re you awake?"

I look around to see who is speaking to me. There is nothing but total darkness.

"Are you awake?" again echoes through my ears, cavernously.

My eyes try to penetrate the void, but to no avail. The darkness is pitch black. I can see nothing.

"Who speaks?" I ask.

A voice answers, "Do not ask any questions. It is important for you to follow my instructions precisely. Your life depends upon it . . . Do you understand me?"

My mind is confused. Am I dead? What happened to me? Where am I? "Yes. I hear you . . . Where am I?"

"You are in the operating room. Do not be alarmed. You are in good hands. We will have you up and around soon. But first we have some important tests to perform. We need your full cooperation . . . Do you understand?"

"I am dizzy, . . . tired, . . . confused, . . . What is happening to me?"

"I will count to three. Tell me if you feel or see anything when I reach three? . . . One . . . Two . . . Three . . ."

"Yes. Yes. I felt a pinch. But I did not see anything . . . What are you doing to me? What happened?"

"I will increase the dosage and try again . . . One . . . Two . . . Three . . ."

"Yes. Yes. I saw sparks. But they quickly disappeared into the darkness."

"Good. Very good. You are responding beautifully to the treatment. Let's try one more time . . ."

A great surge of energy vibrates every fiber in my body. A million specks of light break through the darkness. Each one grows brighter and brighter. My eyes begin to focus. A gray haired man with spectacles on the tip of his nose fills my vision.

"Who are you?" I ask as he twists my head from side to side.

"I am Dr. Malinsky," he answers. "Let me see if you are able to stand?" he implores while sliding my legs over the edge of the table and lifting me gently by the armpits.

I feel faint. My legs wobble at first. But then I manage to steady them. And then walk a few small steps. I smile.

"That's marvelous," he says, placing a screwdriver into my cranial microprocessor to make a final adjustment.

Putric Acid

*L*ook what I have.

A bottle of putric acid. Green liquid acid.

I mix it with my finger.

Mmm. Burns. Burns. But does not hurt. Burns with delicate ecstasy.

Oh, look. Finger gone.

Where go? In acid, maybe?

Try other finger. Mmm. Burns. Burns. But does not hurt. Burns with delicate ecstasy.

Oh, look. Other finger gone too.

I try whole hand. Mmm. Feel spasmodic tickle of acid pinching on my flesh. Has unique sensation, like pins and needles.

Oh, by golly. Look. No hand.

Where go hand? In acid, suppose?

Must try other hand. Feels so good.

In you go, hand. Gently. Ever so gently. Grasp the tingeing, singeing liquid. Bathe in acid so exquisite.

Mmm. Feel so good.

Wiggle, wiggle little hand. Swim around in acid land. Seize the splendor of its power. Mix it, round and round and round.

Mmm. Good. Good.

Oh, by thunder. Look. No hand.

Where go hand? Dissolve in acid?

Try my foot. Both feet, maybe. Twice one foot means double pleasure.

In you go feet. Do not push. Plenty room in bucket. Nice and easy. Do not rush.

Mmm. Feel so sharp. Has my nerves on fine pin cushions.

Little toes wiggle in splendor. One, two, three . . . no more toes.

Oh, by golly. Look.

I sink.

Sink so slowly into the acid. Mmm. Feel spasmodic tickle up and down my spine.

Down and down like elevator. Up to chin in bucket now. Mmm. Never felt so good before.

Down and down and down I go, filling acid bucket to the top.

Mmm. Feel so good.

Mmm. Glob. Glob.

Mmm.

Second Dose

Miracle of Miracles

The earth suddenly begins to move and awakens me from a deep, restful sleep.

It is dark and I can see nothing. The room vibrates and heaves up and down. I am tossed around from one end of the room to the other. I've experienced earthquakes many times before, but nothing like this.

I can hear voices screaming outside. Pandemonium has broken out. Sirens are blasting. Doomsday is here.

But I am trapped. I cannot move. I am trapped in this forsaken room. The walls have collapsed upon me. And I am being crushed to death.

My screams for help are unheard. Terror grips my nerves.

Is there no end to this hideous earthquake? It does not cease. Instead, it grows progressively worse.

The walls keep squeezing me tighter and tighter.

With every ounce of energy in my frail body, I kick and push to keep from being squashed to pulp. But my hands grow weary. I am loosing the battle for survival. Unless a miracle occurs soon, I fear the end is near.

The pipes have broken and water is cascading over me.

But, wait, the water has begun to recede. In fact, it flows across my face over my head, channeling outside.

Thank heavens! . . . That's the way out. The water must flow through a passageway that will lead me out of this darkness into the light. I must follow the stream.

With all my strength, I push, kick and wiggle, contorting every bone in my body. The walls slowly begin to give way and I am able to slither upwards into the narrow passage.

The narrow passage, however, is tight. Somehow, I manage to slide forward. But then my progress comes to a disastrous halt. I am exhausted from the ordeal. I need to rest.

Why doesn't someone help me?

Suddenly, the walls of the passageway begin to collapse. But, miracle of miracles, this time I am propelled forward and ejected from my deadly prison . . . I am saved . . . I am free . . .

Miracle of miracles, someone did hear my prayers.

Gentle hands lift me out of the passage, wipe me down, lift me up by the feet and slap my bare bottom . . .

I cry with joy!

Diary of Dr. Klop and the Secret of Creation

Jan.6: An amazing thing happened today. On feeding my guinea pigs special formula 3077 I noticed a distinct metabolic change. Their heart beat and blood pressure decreased by a factor of two while their motor drives doubled. They also exhibited phenomenal accuracy and speed in running the maze.

Jan.7: Analysis of epidermal tissue gives strong evidence for the formation of additional biological cells. These cells appear to be different from the normal cells . . . I must double check these findings . . . This is fantastic. It means that I may have discovered a way to accelerate the neural network connection between the brain and the internal organs, controlling both the somatic and autonomic systems . . . Indeed, this is most exciting . . .

Jan. 8: Results are identical, as reported yesterday, confirming my diagnostics . . . I, myself, have just ingested 15 grams of formula 3077 and plan to ingest 15 grams of the formula every four hours until I have consumed 90 grams in total . . . Already I notice a surge of intellectual vitality rushing through my body . . . When maximum intelligence is reached I will attempt to solve the riddle of creation: Who created us? Why? And How?

Jan. 9: Things are becoming much clearer and understandable. I am beginning to realiz how simpl evrthng is. Pepl tend to mak things much mor cmplcatd thn tha rely r. Evrthng is so smpl.

Jn. 10: Hv ben abl t solv th riddl f creatn. It is so smpl. Wndr wy we nvr wer abl t solv th prblm befr. Wil writ th ansr tomro aftr I incres th dsg f frmla t twnty grms . . .

J. 11: Amzng hw clr my thnkng hs bcm. Wll tel scrt o creat tmro. j *12*: vrthng prfct. Th scrt f crtn s t ndrstd tha gd xsts n r mnds & th pps f # % s u cn c . . .

j : tdy we x # #!! // %

: ,,, . . . , . . . ,, . .., ,, ...

Figment of Imagination

*B*ill Gladstone rolled his eyes slowly surveying every intricate object in the room. With hands on hips he shook his head up and down, frowning. Then he swept his right arm through the air. "This," he said to Joe Rubio, who lay quietly on the ruffled bed, "All of this is nothing but a figment of my imagination. I dreamt it up. It doesn't exist."

"Yep," said Joe, lazily twisting on his side and propping his chin on a pillow. "I guess you did," he added with a touch of sarcasm in his voice.

"Do you see that chair? . . . That desk? . . . This house? . . . This town? . . . It's all a dream . . . a fantasy. They exist only in my mind." Bill stopped a moment to grasp the significance of his own words. Then he leaned out the window, looked down into the street below, and continued.

"That car, . . . those trees, . . . that beautiful white house across the way," he paused a moment then added, "Only my imagination."

"Well," interjected Joe dubiously. "Go tell Clifford Mangus, who owns that mansion, that it is not real. Tell him that his money is not real. Tell him that his wife and children are not real. Tell him that everything is a mirage."

"But I did dream him up. I created his fortune. I created his oil wells. Everything that exists was created by me . . . I am the center of the universe."

"Now you're getting a bit fantastic, Bill. What makes you think you imagined everything? You may very well be a figment of my imagination. I may have created you in my mind."

"You couldn't have," Bill responded, somewhat perturbed, "That would be illogical. Let me explain . . . If I were a figment of your machination, I would exist only in your mind and would not be aware of my own existence, since I really would not exist . . ."

"So? What is your point?"

"Well now, because I am fully cognizant of my own existence, I must truly be alive . . . My awareness proves my existence."

"Good point."

"I knew I could convince you. I would have it no other way."

"But what does all this mean?"

"It's all very simple and logical . . . When I die, everything around me, in my world, from my viewpoint, dies with me."

"Good point," remarked Joe just before Bill disappeared.

Broodles

*G*ood evening ladies and gentlemen. I'm Bruce Bryzl, the broodler. I have a broodle sent in by a listener. Our panel of experts will try to decipher the broodle by asking questions that can be answered by a simple "yes" or "no." Using twenty or less questions, the panel wins. Otherwise . . . , the . . . broodler . . . wins . . . .

Let's broodle!

One small circle. One large circle around the small circle. A large square around these circles.

We start the questioning with one free guess.

Is it a box of golf balls?

No. No. I'm sorry, it is not a box of golf balls.

Is it a man eating corn on the cob?

No. Sorry, no more free guesses . . . Start the questioning.

Is it solid?

Yes . . . I think so.

Is it movable?

Yes, I'd say it's movable.

Are there several objects in the broodle?

Please explain what you mean.

The two circles, are they movable?

. . . Oh, definitely.

Is that square a separate object also?

Yes . . .

Is the square a living object?

Yes . . .

. . . *Oh, imagine that . . . Well then, are those two circles living objects?*

Yes . . .

Are they doing something that we must find out?

Yes . . .

Is the square a progft?

Yes . . . I think you are close to the answer.

Oh . . . Oh . . . Are those two circles ratfootsdls?

Yes . . .

I GOT IT! It's two ratfootsdls doing handstands on a running progft!

That's absolutely right!

The panel is hot as ever . . .

And remember, dear Martians, feed your ratfootsdls, progfts, foadsrkjs and trsfgazqs Martian Seaweed for better health and bouncing pleasure.

Time to Quelch

"Come. We must greet them," said Manic.

"Do you think they are friendly?" asked Ogar.

"I do not know. They say they come in peace. We will soon find out."

Manic and Ogar chatted nervously as they trotted down the mountain leading the villagers in a procession to meet the strangers that fell out of the sky. The strangers greeted them warmly and prattled incessantly while they were escorted into town.

The procession halted in front of a large puddle of mud that reeked with the smell of camphor. The ceremonies began with the entrance of a dozen beautiful dancing girls. They spun about in the mud with grace and elegance in rhythm with the exotic music. The dancers exited and a group of male dancers charged in with fervor and acrobatics.

Manic gestured to the visitors to enter the mud and dance. The strangers hesitated, but two long-haired visitors entered the mud pool. They danced awkwardly at first, but some villagers joined them and showed them the correct movements. Soon all of the visitors were dancing.

As the music picked up speed and volume, the dancers began to leap high into the air, splashing mud in every direction. How exquisite, the villagers thought. Never before had they experienced such a unique spasmodic dancing. The entire village was enthralled in the frenzy. It was a joyous party.

Finally, Warlit, who stood on a rock high above their heads, waved his hands and shouted. A sudden calmness overtook the villagers. The dancing stopped.

"Ah, it is time to quelch," whispered Ogar to Manic.

"Yes, nothing is better than quelching after dancing."

Warlit scraped a stick against the rock. It burst into flame. He threw it into the mud, which immediately exploded into a sea of flame. The dancers screamed in delight, bathing in the splendor of the quelching. It was so soothing.

When the flames died down the visitors were gone . . . not a minute trace of them was to be found.

"Where have our visitors gone?" asked Ogar. "They were good dancers. They would make such good friends."

"Why did they leave?"

Time in Control

$\mathcal{D}$r. Daniel Abzus looked up from his work-table. His lips stretched in a cynical smile. His eyes squinted in devilish excitement. His laughter pierced the air.

Success. He had finally achieved success in his research. He could control time!

He peered at the computer screen again. There was no doubt about it. One hour, three minutes and two seconds between each blip. The serum worked. It slowed the mouse's heart beat to an almost imperceptible level.

And the mouse returned to normal after the serum wore off . . . with no discernible after effects.

Success! Time was in control!

The needle pinched as he forced the serum into his arm. Then he withdrew the needle and smiled. The world would grow old, but Dr. Abzus would remain young and grow old at an unbelievably slow rate. His experiments proved that in exactly one year, normal time, the drug would wear off. By that time he would have aged only ten minutes. One year compressed into ten minutes . . . The concept was mind boggling . . .

The world accelerated. The sun swept across the sky with supersonic speed. The moon rose and set like a falling star. Day and night flashed on and off. Leaves on the trees grew and shriveled away in seconds.

People shot across the streets like bullets. Cars sped invisibly fast. The sky was sprinkled by rain and snow, on and off, in breathtaking fashion.

Dr. Abzus sensed that he was being moved from room to room, from place to place, from person to person. The dizzy pace made everything a blur. But he did not mind. In fact, he enjoyed every exciting moment. It was fascinating and amusing.

Objects flashed by, like streaks of lightning

It was like a supersonic roller-coaster ride. It was fun and it lasted only ten minutes.

One normal earth year whizzed by . . . Then, suddenly, the earth stopped spinning.

He was lying peacefully on his back on a soft silk bed. It was dark. The air was damp and stuffy, making it difficult to breathe.

He tried to sit up . . . but his head hit the ceiling. He moved his hands and legs . . . but they struck the walls. He screamed as he realized where he was . . . but no one heard him.

Thesis of Ulrick Mnye

*I*NTRODUCTION: The homicidal, schizophrenic tendencies of the inhabitants of the planet Earth, which often result in mass annihilation, has always been of keen interest to the scholars of Mentsza. This thesis attempts to analyze the reasons for such behavior.

ANALYSIS: The behavior pattern of an individual Earthian is amazingly similar to its social group pattern. For example, the individual resorts to violence because it hates its contending counterpart; similarly, a social group hates another social group with the same degree of phrenic behavior. Earthian society is bimodal. It is divided into a "hate" mania and a "love" mania. One either "hates" or "loves." There exists no intermediate sphere of "contentment," as in our own society.

PROBLEM: The problem then is to replace, on the planet Earth, "love" and "hate" with "contentment" in order to transform them into our own equal counterparts.

<u>EXPERIMENT</u>: A granderluch of high-energy photons were radiated on Earth for 24 Earth hours at a gamma speed of 65900 d.fr. According to Barnstrs theory, "Electronic excitations of protoplasmic nerve-centers, if tuned to the proper frequency, will cause a blending of two diverse psychotic conditions producing a single equilibrium state." Thus, the blending of equal amounts of "hate" and "love" should result in the ultimate state of "contentment."

<u>RESULTS</u>: Analysis of the planet Earth after radiation, according to the above dosage procedure, shows conclusively that an equilibrium state of "contentment" has been achieved. However, a small residual amount of "hate" still persists because the "hate" mania was in slight excess over the "love" mania . . .

<u>CONCLUSION</u>: Those few individuals, who remain in the state of "hate," will, undoubtedly, kill the non-resisting, "contented" individuals. In time, the Earth will be occupied by planetarians with a single mania, namely "hate." Further study should be made, in the future, to verify this conclusion.

March for Peace

The police barricaded the street near Central Square, but the barricade did not hold the mob of angry citizens. The police retreated and made a stand at Oak Bridge but were shoved across the bridge. Finally, they made a stand near the Capital Building, but the unruly crowd pushed forward and they were overwhelmed.

Although there was ample warning of the impending protest, the riot police could not control the demonstrators. The city mayor had given strict orders not to use lethal force. Armed only with clubs and tear gas, their lines buckled as the roaring mob of 8,000 swarmed over the barricades.

With full battle cry, the angry citizens wheeled their pitch forks, sledge hammers and crow bars into the police lines. Blood splashed about like red paint. Sirens wailed.

On the verge of defeat, the police panicked, turned tail, and, in full riot gear, retreated as fast as possible. But the mob rushed after them, with banners waving high in the sky, slicing them down like wheat being harvested.

During the retreat, the police fired tear gas at the demonstrators. But the gas was useless. The marchers clubbed their way through each barricade. They kept coming and coming. Each clash was punctuated with bone crunching sounds and ear-piercing screams. Clubs pounded against the riot shields and helmets that offered little protection.

At the steps of the Capital, the police back-up force waited in silence, their hearts palpitating, their adrenaline overflowing. "Remember our orders! Do *not* shoot!" screamed the Commander as he braced for the onslaught. "Do *not* harm the citizens . . . No one wants a massacre."

Waves of people poured into the Capital grounds as the last barricade burst open. Above the moans and groans, the voices of the marchers could be heard singing patriotic songs.

Finally, the frenzy came to an end. The police were totally beaten. Rivers of blood flowed across the lawns, the streets, along the sewers into the drains. A hundred people died that day.

But the citizens had won the battle.

The victors waved their banners high in the air, each emblazoned with a slogan.

"Stop the Killing!"

"We March for Peace!"

Visitors from the Sky

Wee . . . Look at me . . . I shine like a diamond in the sky . . .

Me too . . . Look at me . . .

It's fun to twist and turn as you fall from the heavens.

Yes, indeed. But soon we will land on the Earth and our journey will be over. So enjoy the trip while you can.

I'm lighter than a feather. Every now and then, the wind currents give me a boost upwards.

Me too . . . It's like a roller coaster ride . . . Up and down . . . Up, up, up and down, down, down.

Wow! Did you feel that gust of wind!

It's great . . . Just great . . .

It's exhilarating.

Look at how our dendrites sparkle and glisten . . . like neon lights.

You are indeed beautiful. You sparkle like a hundred fireflies.

You too. And you grow more beautiful with each passing minute. Look at how our dendrites grow, . . . larger and larger as we spiral down.

I was less than a sixteenth of an inch a minute ago, but now I am a quarter inch . . . And I am still growing . . .

This cool, moist atmosphere of Earth is ideally suited to us.

Yes, Earth's atmosphere is perfect.

Watch me spin in circles . . . Wee . . .

I can spin in circles too . . . Watch . . . Wee . . .

Watch me do a somersault . . . One . . . Two . . . Three . . . Over I go . . .

That's great. I must try it . . . One . . . Two . . . Three . . . Wee . . .

Look! I can do a triple somersault . . . Wee . . . Wee . . . Wee . . .

That's great.

We are almost there . . . In another minute or so we will land on the Earth . . . Our trip will be over . . .

Too bad. Just when we were having fun.

Stop playing . . . Look where you are going . . . Be careful not to land in the water . . . or you will dissolve immediately . . .

I can hardly control myself. The wind is strong.

Land over here, near me . . . It looks safe over here.

Yes, I am following your path. The wind has calmed down.

Good. My landing is soft and smooth.

Perfect landing, right next to you.

Oh! No! The Earth is too warm. I am melting . . . Drats! Life is too short.

What Is It?

What is it? Can you guess?
Clue one:
    Useful but useless.
    Good but bad.
    Happy but sad.
    Possible but impossible.
    White but black.
    Rare but common.
    Acid but base.
What is it? Can you guess?
Clue two:
    Dynamic but dull.
    Fast but slow.
    Simple but complicated.
    Fact but fiction.
    Clear but blurred.
    True but false.
What is it? Can you guess?
Clue three:
    New but old.

Clean but dirty.
Silent but noisy.
Hard but soft.
Elegant but sordid.
Rough but smooth.
What is it? Can you guess?
Final clue: (Last chance)
Cruel but peaceful.
Right but wrong.
Ingenious but idiotic.
Sane but mad.
Innocent but guilty.
Meaningful but abstract.
What is it? Can you guess?

For those of you who do not know, the answer is . . .
the answer is . . . the answer is . . . the answer is . . .
detcartsba selat.

*"Bobby, please turn that broken computer off. It never
gives the right answer."*

Third Dose

Mirror Image

*H*e picked it up carefully. It was weightless. It was small, about the size of a baseball . . . It was almost colorless, sort of hazy, sort of glassy, sort of like nothing was really there. But it was there.

John T. Barnobulous, barely five years old, found it on the freshly cut lawn in front of his house.

When he squeezed it, it popped out of his hand like a wet piece of soap and sailed three feet away, landing quietly on the grass. At the same instant, John T. fell backwards landing playfully on the soft grass.

At first he was startled.

Then he smiled and giggled.

He squeezed it again. And again it popped into a perfect arc. And, as if synchronized, John T. popped into the air in the opposite direction. This made him chuckle.

He petted it like a cat, then pulled it cautiously close to the tip of his nose. Softly he said, "My name is John T. Barnobulous. Who are you?"

The ball of massless energy answered, "Oow ra oow? Sulubonrab eeT Noj zee main ym."

John T. laughed.

The glassy plasm giggled.

It was funny . . . It was so funny . . . They laughed together in perfect harmony.

"I'm five years old," John T. said. "How old are you?"

"Oot, dlo sreey vif my," was the answer.

John T. threw his head back and laughed into the sky. He laughed so hard that the ball slipped from his fingers and bounced on the soft grass. He fell backwards bouncing his head in perfect synchronism. It hurt. He rubbed his head and cried with tears streaming down his cheeks.

Vengefully he kicked the image and immediately felt a sharp blow to his stomach that threw him to the ground.

Tears flowed freely.

Angrily he jumped on it, his heels digging deeply into the plasm. He felt a sharp blow to the back of his neck.

He cried tremendously.

Then he stopped abruptly. Picked it up and held it closely to his eyes. There, reflected inside, was the image of a little boy, just like himself, with tears running down his cheeks, crying.

Recipe

What are you cooking?

Quiet . . . Hand me the bottle of greed.

Greed? You're adding greed to the brew?

The recipe calls for two sprinkles of greed. Mix well. Heat to the boiling point. And then add a twang of lust.

Lust? Oh, heaven's all mighty, that is a wicked potion . . . a wicked potion indeed.

Quiet . . . Get me the lust . . . and be quick about it before the soup boils over.

Yes, ma'am.

Now I need three pinches of jealousy . . . There . . . one . . . two . . . three . . . Mmm . . . Smells good. Take a whiff . . . I said, take a whiff!

Yes, ma'am . . . Nnng . . . Achoo . . . Smells real . . . real good.

Now we taste . . . Ssssip . . . Hmm . . . Not right . . . Needs more hate . . . Give me the hate.

Achoo . . . Yes, ma'am.

And maybe a drop or two more of passion of crime . . . There . . . Now take a taste.

Yes, ma'am . . . Ssssip . . . My, that's powerfully powerful. Achoo.

Anger. I forgot the anger. Get me the anger.

Yes, ma'am . . . Achoo . . .

Hurry, hurry, before the brew thickens.

Achoo . . . None left. The bottle is empty . . .

Empty! That can't be. I need anger. Find me another bottle of anger . . . Look in the pantry . . .

Achoo . . . None left . . . Achoo . . . I can't find any anger . . . Achoo . . .

You sneezing idiot. I need anger for my soup. My soup will be ruined without anger. Find me some anger!

Achoo . . . I'm looking. I'm looking . . . No anger here . . .

Find some, you worthless scum! The soup is beginning to gel!

Achoo . . . Can't find any anger . . .

Aaaah! Too Late! My soup has set like plaster of Paris! My ladle is cemented to the pot!

There is no anger.

What's this on the spice shelf? You bumbling moron! Here's the anger! Right here! In front of your nose!

Yes. ma'am . . . Achoo . . . That's anger all right . . .

It's a full bottle, you idiot!

Yes, ma'am. There's plenty of anger around here tonight.

Fantavision

*F*antavision is the latest development to emerge from our research laboratories. There is nothing like it in the world.

You realize, of course, that, as president of Visionary Corporation, my policy is to personally test every new product before manufacturing begins.

Yes, indeed, Mr. Dumounterby, that is why I have brought the prototype model to your office. If you will sit in this chair, I will be glad to demonstrate . . . Very good . . . All the electronic components are contained in this helmet that should fit comfortably over your head . . . See, it fits perfectly.

It's dark in here. I can't see anything.

Press the button on top of the helmet. Sit back. Relax. And watch the show.

This is truly fantastic. I am completely surrounded by a three-dimensional screen. I feel like I am inside the movie.

You *are* inside the movie. In fact you are the main character . . . As the themes flash across the screen, press this front button to make your selection . . . I see you have picked "scary stories." . . . Sit back. Enjoy. And tell me what you see as it happens . . .

Amazing . . . I am in a dark castle. It is cold and damp . . . The wind is howling outside . . . The air has an unusually foul smell . . . like an open sewer . . .

Don't stop. Tell me more.

A bat is circling above my head . . .

Your shivering. Relax. This is only a movie. It is not real.

I know. I know. But the scene is so real . . . Oh my god! . . . The bat suddenly changed into a fully grown man, with a black cape . . . His eyes peer deeply, hypnotically, into my eyes . . . I try to move away, but my body is frozen. I cannot move. I cannot escape.

Heaven help me! He has fangs . . . He slowly approaches . . . I cannot move . . . I am numb . . . He holds my head in his hands, tilts it to the side and bites deeply into my neck . . . Ahhh! . . . I feel the blood being drained from my body . . .

Do not panic. It's all make believe.

It is too real . . . Turn the damn thing off . . . Turn it off!

There, it is off. See everything is normal.

Normal. Normal you say. That was the most frightening experience of my life . . . I am drained . . .

What is this blood dripping from my neck? And how did these two punctures get there? Explain that to me.

Haunt Not the King

"*H*alt! Who goes there, rustling in the darkness?"

"T'is I, the ghost of a mortal being who calls himself by the name chosen by his mother."

"Ghost? I believe in no ghost. Hence, thou canst not be a ghost."

"Perchance, I pray thee, I believe not a word of a man who dost not believe in ghosts. Let me pass."

"Halt! Or I shall shoot with all the King's power vested in the aim of mine shot!"

"Dost thou not know thou canst not kill a ghost?"

"This man can!"

"Ho, ho, thou jests."

"I jest not! Take thineself away or I shall fire into the darkness and end thy blasphemous tongue!"

"Let me pass."

BLAM!

"My Lord, thou dost not jest."

"I jest not! Begone or I shall fire again . . . this time with a prayer that my bullet finds its mark!"

"*I come to haunt the King. He stoleth my birthright. He murdereth my father and my mother, thy true King and Queen. And he murdereth me in my cradle, barely five moons olde. Let me pass.*"

BLAM!

"*Shouldst the King caste eyes upon my specter, he will suredly die, instantly, for I carry the vision of death.*

"Come no furthest! I warn thee."

"*Hold thy fire. Waste not thy bullets. Thou canst not harm a ghost. I shall make my appearance to thee, but I suffer thee not to lay blame that I didst not warn thee, that to caste thine eyes upon me means DEATH.*"

"I fear thee not. I fear no man. I fear no ghost."

"*Then, caste thine eyes and suffer the consequences, you fool.*"

BLAM!

"*Why dost not thou fall down and die?*"

BLAM!

"*Why dost thou not let me take my rightful revenge on thy evil King?*"

"Thou fool, I am the king! I would suredly kill thee twere I not blind! Begone! Thou waseth my time!"

BLAM!

Body of Slime

The air was hot and dry. The sun was unusually bright. Leaves on the trees burned and shriveled

Tiny colonies of mosquitoes formed an orbit over the body that lay face down at the edge of the swamp, with feet buried deeply and body half submerged in the slime. The head protruded upwards as if gasping for air. The body lay deadly still, eyes shut tightly.

The mire carried a peculiar odor of decay. A trained nose would be repulsed by the stench.

Sparkles of light glistened from the buzzing bugs. Some landed and bit hard into the lifeless carcass, but to no avail. The skin was tanned hard by the sun and doubly protected by a thin layer of dried mud. The pickings were poor.

Other hungry animals caught scent of the body and sought after it. But the slime was like quicksand, pulling them down into a deadly trap. They soon scampered away in panic.

A vulture came and circled above for several minutes. Dove down and around. Then decided to land in the field nearby where pickings were better.

The carcass lay motionless.

All was quiet except for the chirping of the crickets and an occasional croak of a frog.

The sun cooked and baked everything in its path that day.

A tiny black cloud moved swiftly across the sky bringing a little bit of relief when it sprinkled a teasing trace of rain across the arid terrain. The moisture quickly steamed off.

Then the silence was broken by the barking of dogs and a voice shouting in the distance.

Abruptly the eyes of the lifeless body snapped open. The head popped up and out. Then the corpse rose from the dead sleep and bounded out of the mire in a hellish manner, squealing in a most ferocious manner, and running as fast as his feet could carry him directly to the voice that called.

Only the wooden fence stopped the monster from escaping and the dogs from attacking.

"Calm down!" farmer Jones shouted at the dogs.

"And you calm down too!" he shouted to his prized jumbo pig as he poured a huge bucket of the food scrap into the trough in the pen.

When Luigi Fought
the Monster

*L*uigi cringed with fear before stepping into the boxing ring. "How did he get into this mess?" he asked himself agonizingly.

Luigi was the heavyweight champion of the world, successfully defending his title thirty-five times by knockouts. The Solarians challenged him to fight their champion. Luigi was amused because the Solarians were weak neophytes. Not one was taller than five feet nor heavier than ninety pounds. Luigi accepted the challenge blindly without bothering to read the details of the contract. He did not know that he had actually agreed to fight a mechanical monster built by the Solarians.

Oblivious to the contract details, Luigi spent the month resting in the mountains, away from the press, television, radio and people. He wanted peace and quiet.

Fight day finally came. Thousands of people crowded the arena. Millions tuned their television to the fight channel.

When Luigi stepped into the ring he was flabbergasted to see a metal monster in the diagonal corner. He fumed with rage. "What is this?" he shouted. "I signed to fight a Solarian, not a machine!" But it was too late to complain. The contract was signed. Everyone knew about the contract, except Luigi and his trainer . . . But now they knew . . . And Luigi was frightened.

The monster weighed at least five hundred pounds. It reacted with precision and speed. Computer-wise, it was ingenious. Mechanically, it was perfect. Physically it was superhuman.

Poor Luigi. Tears clouded his vision, sober tears of realization.

Little Luigirina ran to her daddy, hugged him and kissed him, her usual ritual before each fight. "Win this fight for me, daddy," she said, popping her bubble gum in his face and sticking a wad on his glove for good luck.

Luigi smiled bravely. "Of course," he said, fearfully.

The bell rang. The metal monster charged forward. Luigi took two bold steps forward, gathered his courage, swung a fist into the stomach of the monster, and ducked low to the ground. The monster stopped dead, swayed, teetered and tottered, and fell to the ground with a resounding thud.

The crowd roared. The Solarians were silently stupefied.

Luigirina jumped into the ring, quietly removed her bubble gum from the monster where it covered a tiny air hole.

And she blew another bubble.

Go to Hell

*H*ey, where do you think you're going?

Why, to heaven, of course.

Let me see your passport.

. . . Passport? I don't have a passport.

You have to have a passport to get in to Heaven . . . What's your name? I'll see if you're in the listed in the Book.

Beelzebub.

. . . Oh, it's you again. How many times must I tell you that you can't get into Heaven without a passport? Changing your shape doesn't qualify.

I've done the best I could, Peter. I've completely reformed. I've given up cursing and swearing. I no longer smoke nor drink. I've been honest, and kind, and trustworthy, and clean. I donate to the poor. I tend to the sick.

Too late. The Good Book says your accommodations are downstairs in the bargain basement, not upstairs in the penthouse.

. . . Tell you what I'll do. I will sign a pledge in blood swearing that I will never sin again, as long as I live.

Nice try, Beelzy, but you don't have any blood . . .
And your dead, not alive.

Just tell me one thing, Peter. What must I do to get better accommodations? It's as hot as Hell downstairs. I can't stand the heat anymore. Why am I being discriminated against? Why?

. . . You curse too much.

Not any more. I've given up cursing.

. . . You're holding up the line.

There's no justice anymore.

Get out! . . . Go back to Hell! . . . Guards! . . .
Guards! . . . Guardian Angels!

I'm going. I'm going. Don't get excited.

Guards!

I'm going . . . Guess I'll have to pray some more. Must never give up faith. Someday I will qualify for Heaven.

Guards, throw this liar out of here!

Back to Hell . . . Must pray some more . . .

Hmm . . . Finally got rid of the him . . . What's this he dropped on the ground? . . . A prayer book? . . . The cover says "Bible." Let's see what's printed inside . . . Ow! . . . It's on fire! . . . Burnt my fingers . . . What a clever devil he is. He often pretends to be a Christian . . . like so many other people I know.

Homework Subject

I strongest man in world.

Perchance, 'tis so that you are, but what good can brute strength have in a world where the mightiest men are the thinkers?

I kill all. I strong. No stronger than I.

I fully realize that you are a relegate of the past and that you are here by no desire of your own. However, the situation remains as is and, I dare say, you must make an adjustment to it or suffer the undue consequences.

You talk like chicken. Gabble. Gabble. Gabble . . . Why no you fight? I king of all men. I strong.

Sir, I must implore you to desist from squeezing my arm.

No muscle. Chicken bone. You feel like chicken and you sound like chicken.

Heaven on Earth, why did I ever pick you as my subject for theoretical study of ancient anthropology? I'll surely flunk the course now.

Let me see teeth.

My dear man, take your hands off my face. Stop pulling my lips. That hurts.

Horse have better teeth.

Sit down in this chair while I get my notepad. I have a lot of questions to ask you.

How I get here?

I projected you through the time tunnel.

Ugh. You crazy. No make sense.

I have many questions to ask you. Time is short before you are automatically projected back. So, please, answer my questions carefully.

I hungry. Need food.

Here, swallow these. They're food pills, equivalent to a full course turkey dinner with stuffing and vegetables. Take them.

No eat pebbles. Pebbles no good. Make sick.

Let me show you . . . See . . . Tastes good . . . Real good . . . My stomach is full . . . Tastes like turkey . . . Delicious . . . Here . . . Eat . . . And then drink this glass of triply-distilled water . . .

You crazy man . . . I hungry . . . Need meat . . . Not stones . . .

I have no meat. In the Modern Age, where you are now projected, we eat purified food, purified by radiation, dehydration and sanitation. These pills are germ free, microbe free, poison free . . . Stop pulling my arm . . .

Need food . . . You sound like chicken. You feel like chicken. Mmm . . . You taste like chicken.

Image Pills

*T*he bell rang but thrice. Bayhee jumped up from his relaxachair, where he was deeply absorbed in reading a thrilling science-fiction "feelie." Three bells meant the postman.

The package was small. It contained something he wanted for many years, a rare, high priced chemical from Centrabolidt. It was sold only to members of the carbonaceous family because it was known to alter the appearance of these species . . . And there it was, after five long years of waiting.

Bayhee ran to the antiseptic room where he hastily tore the wrapping from the package. Inside the plastic box was a tiny bottle containing ten red tablets, and a sheet of instructions. Full of excitement, he read the instructions rapidly, but carefully, especially the paragraph that read, "The subject must concentrate deeply and precisely until able to produce, in his conscious mind, the exact image desired. When image control has been established, the subject may evaluate the success of the experiment by devouring one tablet of Drezb. If bodily changes are satisfactory, one can then devour the next tablet, and the next in cautious succession until the desired result is obtained . . . The manufacturers of Drezb assume no responsibility for any effects of this drug. By law, no refills and no refunds are permitted."

Bayhee looked into the full-length mirror to see his ugly self for the last time. Carrot nose. Owl eyes. Elephant ears. Skeleton frame. Leathery skin. Protruding elbows. Doorknob knees. Duck feet. But not for long.

He closed his eyes tightly, projecting the vision of his future self. The image was perfect. He burned the image into his head.

Nervously, he removed one tablet from the bottle, placed it carefully on his tongue and swallowed. It burned its way to his stomach, like a hot coal from hell. But somehow the burning was euphoric.

He peeked through his eyelids and witnessed a slow transformation. The pills were working. Following the directions explicitly, he swallowed another and another and another, until the bottle was empty.

He was truly handsome. His image was perfect in every detail.

He was at peace with himself. Proud to be alive.

Although his family and friends saw no physical change, they were pleased to see that Bayhee was now happy.

Super-Ego Syndrome

D*ay 1*: Arrived safely on Star Silicon . . . Cordially greeted by hosts . . . Escorted through Granita, the capital city . . . Toured the villages and the occupational centers . . .

Day 2: Previous expeditions reported that the Siliconians suffer from super-ego syndrome . . . An incident occurred today to verify the prognosis . . . On the way to the Intergalactic Council Meeting, I was deliberately escorted through a natural cave of red hot coals. My escort, a short crystalline Siliconian, who called himself Jalub, was not burned in the slightest because his silicon composition could tolerate such temperatures . . . My skin burned somewhat in spite of the solar-screen salve I had applied earlier in anticipation of something like this . . . The egometer in my utility belt, secretly focused on Jalub, registered 100 . . . the maximum reading . . .

Day 3: Another incident occurred today to confirm the seriousness of the situation . . . During the evening banquet,

I was served a beverage of flaming hot oil. The Siliconians gulped the fiery liquid with expressions of superiority that words cannot describe. They took special delight at my feeble excuses for not imbibing . . . The egometer pegged to maximum . . .

Day 4: A terrible accident happened today. Our transportation vehicle spun out of control and crashed in a ravine. All passengers, myself and three Siliconian ambassadors, were seriously hurt. I suffered lacerations of the face, black eyes and a broken leg. All others have fractured arms, legs and heads.

Day 11: I am recuperating from the accident. The swelling in my face has receded, the black eyes are gone, my leg is in a cast but I am able to walk with crutches . . .

Day 18: Visited by the Siliconian ambassadors who were in the accident . . . Evidently they do not heal . . . Their fractures are permanent, like broken glass . . . Their damaged limbs are missing and cannot be recrystallized, nor fused back together . . . They were astonished to see that I am self-healing . . . Egometer registered very low . . . Super-ego syndrome has completely disappeared . . . Epidemic abated . . . Crisis over . . . Project completed . . .

Fourth Dose

The Trial of
Misr Masr

*P*rosecutor: You claim you were sane at the time and had complete control of your senses?

Misr Masr: That's right. And I'd do it again.

Prosecutor: Do you realize the seriousness of your crime?

Defender: Objection, your honor. The act in question has not been determined to be a crime. That's for the jury to decide.

Judge: Objection sustained. The prosecutor must refrain from prejudging the situation.

Prosecutor: Sorry, your honor . . . Tell us again, exactly what happened.

Misr Masr: As I said before, I was reading the newspaper in the kitchen, having breakfast, when it crashed through the ceiling and landed on the rug. A tiny door opened and a dozen bug-like creatures came prancing out of the blasted thing . . .

Prosecutor: The thing was obviously a spaceship.

Misr Masr: Yes, . . . but I didn't know that at the time. It startled me. I was frightened.

Prosecutor: Describe these bug-like creatures.

Misr Masr: They were about a half inch tall, with silvery skin. Antennae jutted out of their glassy heads. Their muscles bulged grotesquely. Ugly veins ran across their bodies.

Prosecutor: Spacesuits . . . Obviously . . .

Misr Masr: I had no way of knowing that at the time.

Prosecutor: Continue. Then what happened?

Misr Masr: They carried guns . . . They pointed them at me. I was sure they were going to fire them . . .

Prosecutor: And then?

Misr Masr: I was frightened. I never saw anything like that before. Their guns were pointing at me . . . I had to act fast.

Prosecutor: What did you do?

Misr Masr: I swatted them with the newspaper.

Prosecutor: Aha! Because you were frightened, you swatted them with your newspaper! You deliberately killed them, all of them . . . And then what did you do?"

Misr Masr: I trampled the rocketship into the ground.

Prosecutor: Deliberate murder! . . . That was the first spaceship from Earth to Pluto . . . You killed them all . . . Murderer!

Misr Masr: Your honor, I demand a new trial with a Plutonian judge and a Plutonian jury. You Earthlings don't understand.

Transformation

$\mathcal{M}$y eyes glow with feverish excitement, for I hold in my hands the elixir destined to give eternal life. Years of deep scientific study were devoted to perfecting the elixir. Now it is ready for final testing. One whiff will transform my frail human body into an immortal spirit, impervious to disease and pestilence.

It is fluid and yet it is not fluid. See how it foams over the test tube, ever so lazily. Then down upon my hand. Across my wrist. So cool . . . And yet it burns with exquisite sensation.

Some flows over the rim, breaking from the main stream, directly down to the floor forming a small, misty fog around my feet.

I spy a rodent running across the floor. What an ugly creature. But, alas, it stupidly wanders into my splendiferous mixture of gaseous foam that oozes across the floor. A bubble of the white foamy vapor encircles the rodent. And slowly fades into the nostrils of the beseeched animal.

Curses, I know not what effect the elixir will have on a mouse. The formula is based on the human genetic code. This is an unfortunate accident that I had not anticipated.

Before my eyes I witness a grotesque horror, enough to turn anyone grey. Something is wrong. Something is drastically wrong. I must quickly prepare an antidote.

Where are my notes? Where are my reading glasses?

Too late. My head is starting to spin.

My eyes tear and burn deeply as they desperately try to focus on a most unbelievable sight. The rodent squirms, and kicks, and shrieks, and spins upon its back in gurgling circles. With each revolution it grows in size. Bigger and bigger. Faster and faster.

Its legs sprout like trees. Its tail shrinks to nothing. Its grey skin turns pink. Truly pink. Heavens above, it gains stature greater than I.

It grows so huge.

It towers high above me.

What is that, that it holds perched between its limbs? A test tube . . . with white foaming, odorous, fluid liquid, . . . with vapors that pour down and hover around me.

My mind is confused by the foul smelling cloud that engulfs me. My body is stifled. The vapors circle my grey self, tail, whiskers and all.

Concerto for Piano

*H*is fingers struck the ivory keys with sharpness and precision. In response, the felt hammers stamped the strings of the grand piano, producing a resonating sound that echoed throughout the hall.

The vibrations were perfection in harmony and synchronism.

As his fingers danced across the keyboard, the individual tones blended into a magnificent display of mellifluous music never before heard by people on Earth.

This was different.

Fuller.

Richer.

Vigorous.

Vibrant.

Suddenly, it was soft . . . soothing . . . poetic . . . soulful . . . like colorful mountains . . . birds . . . and flowers . . .

The music flowed like water splashing against some rocks that jutted out in the middle of a stream. Then it magically changed into clouds that flowed lazily across the sky.

The notes were alive.

Then, without warning, the sounds transformed into a staccato of bellowing low notes, punctuated with a series of high notes, leading to a thundering crescendo.

The piano vibrated . . . then bounced . . . and seemed to come alive . . . as the pianist pushed himself, with both hands and feet, far away from the piano, in utter amazement.

The keys played by themselves . . .

Faster and faster.

The piano danced in devilish merriment.

Then it began to bend, like rubber, as it danced.

The audience was spellbound. The music was magnificent. The sounds were unique, discordant and melodious.

The keyboard began to wave . . . up and down . . . faster and faster . . . higher and higher . . .

The piano reached such tremendous heights of emotion that it suddenly exploded into a thousand pieces as it played the final notes of the concerto.

The audience sighed . . . then rose to a standing ovation as they clapped thunderously.

Never again will such artistic music be heard . . . or seen.

Another Dimension

$\mathcal{M}$arlo slid over to Sprig, peeked across his shoulder at the paper Sprig was so intently viewing. "What are you reading?" he asked inquisitively.

Sprig was startled by the unexpected voice. "Oh . . . a science-fiction story . . . about another world that has a third dimension."

"Three dimensions? What's a third dimension?" Marlo puzzled.

"Something called depth," Sprig replied.

Marlo shrugged. "Depth? What's depth?" he asked.

"Well, its very complicated," Sprig mulled, "but let me try to explain it to you . . . A point in space represents the zero dimension . . . By moving the point forward we form a line . . . The line exists in one dimension . . . Do you understand that?"

Marlo nodded.

Sprig continued, "Now let's move the line sideways forming a plane . . . The plane lies in two dimensions . . . Just like the two-dimensional world we live in today . . .

A world with only length and width . . ." He paused, carefully contemplating his thoughts.

"Yes, yes, go on," urged Marlo.

"Let me try to demonstrate."

Sprig spun in planar circles while he tried to think of a simple explanation, a most challenging task.

"First, we draw a straight line like this," he said, gliding forward smoothly. Then he spun completely around and glided back over the line to the middle.

"Now, we draw a second line . . . But this line we draw perpendicular to the first line . . . Like this . . ."

He continued, "Although each line has only one dimension, the two lines, together, lie in a two-dimension world . . ."

"Yes, yes." Marlo interrupted. "I understand. But what is depth?"

"You must use all the power of your imagination to visualize the third dimension," cautioned Sprig. ". . . Imagine another plane, different from the plane we live in . . . Now turn this plane so it is perpendicular to our planar world . . . Each plane has only two dimensions . . . but, together, they lie in a three-dimensional world. The extra dimension is called . . . depth . . ."

Marlo shrugged his head. "How fantastic!"

"It's only science fiction," added Sprig as he darted away in spiraling circles.

Perspective

$\mathcal{H}$e looked into the mirror sternly and critically. With bony fingers he pawed at his baggy face. His cheeks sagged. His chin jutted out awkwardly. His nose was crooked. His eyes were bloodshot with rivers of red veins crisscrossing the marbleized whites. There was no doubt, he said to himself, he is the ugliest man on Earth.

He smashed his hairy fists against the mirror and cried aloud.

His home was an old mansion outside the village, inherited from his parents who died twenty years ago leaving him ample money. He dreaded going into the village for food and clothing. The townspeople would curse him. And the children would throw sticks and stones, and call him the "bogey man."

The only one who would sell him food and clothing was old man Pirogi. That was because Pirogi was a miser who loved money more than he hated ugliness. Pirogi charged him outrageous prices for the rotten food and clothing that no one else wanted.

He did not object to the prices, for his parents left him a small fortune, but what hurt the most was a lack of friends and a lack of respect.

One day Pirogi, after much haggling and persuasive salesmanship, coerced him into purchasing a bottle of sulfur water, reputed to possess curative properties. The price was indeed outrageous.

He slept soundly that night after drinking the entire bottle of the sulfur water. His dreams were pleasant. He dreamt of flowers, colorful flowers, red, blue, yellow, white, . . . each with its own unique, fragrance . . . His lungs bathed in the aroma . . . His entire body experienced a magical, soothing massage . . . . Everything was peaceful . . . restful . . . tranquil . . .

In the morning he looked into the mirror and could not believe what he saw . . . His scars and wrinkles were gone. His jutting chin, baggy eyes and crooked nose were molded into perfect harmony. His face was smooth. His hands were soft. His back was straight. His shoulders were square. He was handsome.

He ran to the village. He was so happy he laughed.

"Are these the same people?" he asked himself. "Yes, they are. But I never noticed their deformities before. They are wrinkled. They have scars. They walk crooked. There faces are twisted . . ."

"Everyone is so ugly," he thought, and went back home.

Egotistical Psychosis

I am prOsh. I am from Scorpius, a planet in Galaxy NG.

How did you get here? You speak our language so fluently.

Your emanations contain nothing more than a compilation of rhythmic, barbaric jocular that can be emulated by any simple moron. As for my mode of transportation, I find no suitable words in your inferior language to express the psYch process that has enabled me to be the first to visit this forsaken, hellish planet. Suffice to say that I have traveled by psych-warp . . . . Show me your barren planet . . .

. . . These are our Agricultural Synthetic Food Plants . . . capable of growing fifty pound apples and four-foot bananas . . . And this, as our jet turns to the left, is our Unitized Plasmatic Hospital, capable of synthesizing bone, internal organs and blood plasma from vegetable matter . . . On the right is our Atomic Car Assembly Line, producing crash proof automobiles with top speeds of 500 kilometers per hour . . .

Primitive. Definitely primitive.

. . . We are now traveling through the Nuclear Proto Power Plant, which provides a superabundance of electricity for all our manufacturing and home needs.

Electricity? Simply barbaric. Crude, wasteful and inferior.

Our Clothing Center is automatic, operated solely by robots.

Materialistic clothes? How primordial. How utterly backward. I must say your world is frightfully materialistic. So imperfect. So basically undeveloped. I find it difficult to believe that I am witnessing such an unrefined civilization. I begin to doubt that we are of the same species even though we look alike in all physical appearances . . . Mentally you are lunatic imbeciles, priding yourselves on a materialistic world. When will you learn that perfection in man can only be achieved by proper mental, psychical and philosophical attainment?

. . . But we are happy.

How can you be happy? To be happy you must live in a psychic world and not a materialistic world. When will you Earthlings ever learn the truth?

. . . Earthlings?

Is this not Earth, the third planet from the Sun?

. . . Indeed not. This is your Id, the world of your inner subconsciousness.

The Suitcase

Brad Brodnick put his suitcase down alongside his seat and walked over to the water fountain in the train station. He put his mouth near the spout and stood for a brief moment enjoying the cool water as it trickled down his throat. He walked back to his seat and picked up his suitcase.

A short cab ride brought him to his apartment. He threw his suitcase on the bed. A soft, low, wailing sound perked his attention. But it quickly stopped.

Exhausted from the trip, Brad went into the bathroom and drenched his face with refreshing water.

A faint scratching sound seemed to emanate from the other room . . . Brad stopped washing. With water dripping from his face, he listened intently . . .

The sound ceased. His eyes surveyed the bedroom. Everything appeared normal. Nothing was out of order.

He shrugged, shook his head, and went back into the bathroom.

Suddenly, the soft wailing sound permeated the silence again, but instantly stopped.

Brad scurried into the bedroom. "Did the wailing come from inside the suitcase?" he thought to himself.

He put his hand on the case. Then he noticed it wasn't his. He had the wrong suitcase. The cases must have been mixed at the train station.

Brad flipped open the lid.

A hairy, green animal popped up, like a jack-in-the-box. It was the size of a monkey with fanged teeth and pig nostrils. It snarled ferociously at him, and scratched the air with razor sharp claws.

Brad jumped backwards, almost falling over his own feet.

The beast leaped out of the case, bounded across the room and sprung through the open bedroom window into the street below, screeching loudly in the process.

Suddenly, a short, plump man, no more than five feet tall, appeared in the middle of the room. He was obviously irate as he shouted, "You idiot! Why did you let the veebleforsh out of the case? I'll never catch him in the time warp now!" The short, plump man disappeared as mysteriously as he appeared.

The room stood quiet. Brad, still dazed, stared into space, wondering what had happened.

Dinner

"**M**mm," Josephine Accipiter muttered to herself. "Delicious. So tender and delicate . . . I have not had a meal so delicious in my entire life . . . These fresh bodies are so much better than the old dried up ones I've been eating lately."

She chewed a chunk of pink flesh from one of the legs and gulped it down. The saliva drooled from her mouth onto the ground, mixing with the pool of blood already there.

The air was deadly quiet . . . Her eyes darted from side to side in a frenzy, ensuring that no one else was watching or waiting. Not a living creature was to be seen.

She tore into the gizzards, swallowing quickly, viciously and stealthily. The gizzards were the caviar. So sinfully tasty . . . Then she gnawed the neck.

Josephine was a member of the Accipiter family, a unique family, highly respected throughout the entire world. In fact, so respected, that they have received special consideration from many ruling bodies and philanthropic organizations.

Unfortunately, each member of the Accipiter family is cursed with a severe allergic condition that could be fatal if precautions were not taken. The condition is inherited and there is no known cure. Only by exercising extreme caution can this family survive on earth. In fact, at this very moment, there are very few living members remaining.

The sun was bright. There was not a single cloud in the sky. This fateful combination of nature, in actuality, steamed and cooked the carcass of the victim, bringing out the full flavor. In essence, the prey basked in a hot gravy of fresh blood, a connoisseur's delight.

"One more bite," Josephine reveled, even though she had already eaten her fill and could hardly devour another morsel.

"I do not know when I will find such a tasty animal again."

She tore into the brain, slobbering and belching as she completed her feast . . . So satiated with food, she could hardly hold back from regurgitating.

Not a single piece of flesh could be found.

Only the bones of the field mouse, licked clean, remained.

"A good days kill," she said to herself, as she flapped her wings in majesty and flew high into the sky on direct route to her nest, to feed her newly hatched brood.

Murder

"No. No. I can't!"

"Why can't you?"

"I just can't," Ralph Walters responded sardonically.

"It's only a robotron," Karl Manning said, urging Walters to change his mind. "It must be either repaired or disposed. But we must act immediately."

"I can't .... Believe me, I just can't," cried Walters.

"It's a danger to your life and the lives of everyone around here. When the brain center of a robotron burns out, the robotron can no longer control its functions. There is no way of telling what it will do. Burn out is equivalent to insanity. It cannot be trusted. The central brain unit must be replaced or the robot must be disposed."

"Replacing the brain unit will destroy all previous memory. He will no longer be the robot I once knew," Walters lamented.

"Then get rid of it before it hurts someone."

The robotron lay in the corner of the room, giggling and swaying from side to side, smashing its head against the wall.

"I can't dispose it," Walters kept reiterating.

"We must take it to the Central Disposal Center," Manning urged passionately.

"That would be murder, plain murder," Walters sobbed.

"Nonsense. Disposing a robot isn't murder. Robots are disposed every day. There is no difference between disposing a worn out robot than disposing a worn out washing machine or a worn out television set."

"But this *is* different," pleaded Walters.

"How is it different? . . . All robots are alike . . . They have no feelings . . . They are mechanical protoplasms . . . They are manufactured . . . They wear out . . . And when they wear out, they must be disposed . . . , like garbage."

"No. No."

"You must get rid of it!" Manning screamed, loosing patience and grabbing Walters by the cheeks and shaking him fiercely. "Look at it kicking wildly on the floor . . . It's out of control . . . It's downright dangerous!"

"Oh god!" Manning screamed as Walters' face crumbled under the pressure of his hands, revealing a metallic interior.

"I can't," said the metal head. "The robotron is my FATHER . . ."

Back to Earth

*T*hey took one more look at the majestic white building before straggling up the hill to investigate. The black iron gate was open. So the crew entered.

They walked through the hallway, following the sounds of voices that came from a room at the far end of the corridor. Men and women sat at wooden tables, eating and chattering noisily.

A tall, neatly dressed man wearing a beard and a top hat approached them and said, "I am Abraham Lincoln. Welcome to my home."

The captain smiled, extended his hand, and replied, "I am Captain Clayton Jones from Philadelphia, Pennsylvania . . . Earth. Due to a faulty computer, we have been lost for three years, and have just now landed safely on your planet . . . Would you be so kind to tell us where we are?"

"You are in the White House in Washington, D.C." the tall man responded.

The crew were stunned. "How can that be?" the captain puzzled. "There are no other buildings nearby . . . What year is it?"

"Today is June 15, 1861," Abraham Lincoln answered.

"No it isn't!" shouted a cigar smoking, bearded man in a blue uniform. "You know damn well today is June 3, 1864."

"Who are you?" the captain asked.

"I am General Ulysses S. Grant, Commander of the Union Army," the cigar smoker shouted, drawing out his sword and brandishing it through the air.

The captain scratched his head. "What happened to the Earth while we were lost in space?" he asked.

"The Earth exploded," interrupted another person. "There is nothing left of the Earth. Doomsday came. And doomsday went. And the cat jumped over the moon."

"And the fiddle ran away with the spoon . . ." screeched another.

Suddenly the hall exploded with laughter. The rafters trembled with shouts and screams. People jumped up from their seats, knocking over the tables. They swarmed around the crew and lifted them on their shoulders, high into the air.

At first they were frightened, but slowly the crew began to see the novelty of the situation, and they joined the laughter.

"Captain, I think I know where we are," Lieutenant Jodee said as he was jostled about. "We are in an insane asylum."

Fifth Dose

The Black Knight

They lifted him gently onto his white horse. The armor was heavy. Heavy, indeed. Four men in all lifted the White Knight onto his armored horse.

Little Billy Bantor filled his six-year-old lungs with air. It was stuffy inside the steel helmet, and the air reeked with perspiration.

Slowly he grasped the reins through his steel gloves. With his other hand he took hold of the ten-foot wooden lance. With his shielded elbow he tapped the handle of golden sword twice to make certain that it was secure in its holder along the side of the horse. Through the narrow slits in the helmet he peered down, and sighed with assurance that his chain-and-ball was in place.

Then his eyes scanned across the battlefield. There on the other side of the field, stood the Black Knight, the terror of the common people, the scourge of the world. The Black Knight pulled back on the reins, his horse kicking his front legs high in the air and braying.

Billy gritted his teeth in hate, and spat. Tiny beads of sweat ran down his face. He was scared.

This was a battle to the death.

Only one would survive.

Only one victor.

Only one loser.

He charged forward. The Black Knight charged forward. They raced at each other with their lances pointing to the heavens. As they approached within striking distance, they slowly lowered their weapons in position for the kill.

But the lance was too heavy, too heavy to hold straight. He was so small, and the lance was so big. It was much too heavy.

It slipped and fell to the ground.

The big Black Knight charged down upon him. The lance struck him squarely in the chest, knocking him off the steed. He was helpless. The heavy armor anchored him to the ground.

The Black Knight reined his horse around and charged full force for the final kill. The lance pierced through his metal shield and through his heart. Billy screamed and screamed.

His mother shook her head pitifully, as she watched him twist and turn in painful agony. Then she said, "Billy, that's enough. Why do you scream like that? Please put your toy soldiers away."

Questions

Who created the stars? Who is god? Who created god? How big is the universe? Why is the sun hot? Why is the moon bright at night? Why is the world round? Why do fish swim? Why do birds fly? What makes an airplane fly? Why don't thing fall up instead of down? Why does it rain?

Shut up.

Who am I? Where am I? What am I? Where did I come from? Why must I eat? Why must I sleep? Why do I dream? Why do I have two eyes? Why do I have two arms, two hands, two legs, two feet? Why do I laugh? Why do I cry? Why do I feel pain? Why do I bleed? Why is blood red? How do I heal? Why do I ask these questions?

Shut up.

How many people live on the earth? Why do they speak different languages? Why are their skins different colors? Why do they kill each other?

Shut up.

What is color? Why does red feel warm and blue feel cold? Do people see the same colors? Do cats see colors? How many different colors are there?

Shut up.

Why is fire hot? Why is ice cold? Why is water wet? Why are solids hard? What is a molecule? What is an electron? Why does one plus one equal two? Why does one plus two equal three? Who invented the straight pin?

Shut up.

What is time? How do I waste your time? Why can't I see time? How does time fly? Where does time go? How can I save time? Can you spend some time with me?

Shut up.

Why do you tell me to shut up? Why are you getting out of your chair? Why are you going over to the desk? What are you looking for? Why are you putting your hand inside the drawer? Why are you holding a gun? What are you going to do with the gun? Why do you pull the trigger?

Bang!

Why are you lying on the floor? Why can't you get up?

Why? Tell me why?

Why?

Philosophically Speaking

$\mathcal{P}$rometheus was a mouse. But you wouldn't know it if you met him. He looked like a mouse. He smelled like a mouse. He squeaked like a mouse. But he didn't act like a mouse.

You see, Prometheus had a philosophy. That's what made him different from all the other mice.

His philosophy was very simple. He believed that the whole world was merely a figment of his imagination. Nothing really existed. Everything was a dream . . . sometimes a good dream and sometimes a bad dream.

With this philosophy Prometheus became fearless. He reasoned that if everything were merely a figment of his subconscious mind then there is nothing to fear. Thus, armed with such ideas, he found no reason to lurk in the dark catacombs of the woodwork like other fearful mice. Instead, he boldly lived in the beautiful open air filled with sunshine and fresh smelling flowers.

Food was no problem. Since everything was imagined he simply ate the food that appeared in his dreams.

People were astounded by the friendly audacity of the rodent, and came to enjoy his daily visits to the park where he was handsomely fed leftovers and occasionally fresh, lean meat.

At the same time, there lived a cat named Androcoles who prided himself on his prowess and practicality. He felt that all problems in life have a *practical* solution.

It was fate that brought Prometheus and Androcoles together.

The day was unusually hot. Androcoles had not eaten for a day because his usual garbage delicatessen had nothing edible to offer that morning. So he decided to try the park, instead. Prometheus, on the other hand, went about his daily ritual of dining in the park with his human friends. Thus, by accident, they met on the edge of the pond where both went to drink.

"By gad," said Androcoles, the cat, "you're a mouse. Why, in heavens' name don't you run away? Aren't you afraid of me?"

"Of course not," answered Prometheus, the mouse, "you are merely a figment of my imagination. I dreamt you up. You do not really exist. So why should I be afraid?"

"That's an odd philosophy," queried Androcoles. "Then explain this." Without warning, he seized the mouse and swallowed him.

As darkness engulfed him, Prometheus said to himself, "This cannot be real . . . This is just another bad dream."

Dinner Party

"*P*ass the fried turkey legs!" cried Bobbs as he bounced in his seat, ravenously hungry and excited.

"I'll have another cup!" shouted April, pointing to the teapot that jiggled, steamed and whistled on the hotplate.

"Where's the cheese?" asked Mousey as he fell backward in his chair, somersaulting across the floor.

Sourpuss shoveled a tablespoon of blueberries in his mouth, thumbed his nose, wiggled his ears and stuck out his purple tongue.

No one noticed a shiny object fall from the sky and settle in the trees nearby . . .

The party was going in grand style. Everyone was having a splendid time. They were too busy eating and cajoling to notice anything out of the ordinary.

Racasac fiddled an unharmonious tune. The thunderous ovation he received compelled him to screech louder, spine-chilling. Entranced by the merriment, Bellisha danced the jig on one foot. Soon they all were dancing, not in rhythm but in extemporaneous rhapsody.

No one noticed several creatures descend from the shiny object . . .

They were too busy throwing spoons and making faces at each other. The party reached a state of confusion and pandemonium. Crumpets flew through the air. Tea rivered across the white tablecloth onto the ground.

No one noticed the creatures approaching, as Sourpuss pulled the hat down over Racasac's eyes and shouted in his ears. They screamed with delight and pounded the table, creating thundering sounds.

No one noticed how quickly Mousey disappeared, as April balanced the ketchup bottle on her nose and walked across the table with her hands stretched out like wings.

No one noticed that Bobbs and Bellisha were gone, as Racasac accidentally stepped on his fiddle, mashing into the ground.

No one noticed when April bounded out of sight.

No one noticed that Racasac vanished.

No one noticed the party was over.

No one remained.

And no one noticed the creatures licking their lips.

The Old Mansion

*T*he old mansion stood on the hill above the village ever since anyone could remember. One might venture to say that it seemed to have grown out of the ground.

It was much taller than it was wide or long, . . . much, much taller, with big, long windows framed in withering oak. The roof was very steep and somewhat oriental in design, with large eaves that unbalanced the house.

No one ever saw any of the people who lived inside. The door was always locked. Sometimes mischievous children would knock on the big oak door, and from within a horrible voice would shout, "Go away!"

Salesmen, postmen, passing strangers, cats and dogs would avoid the house. It gave one the shivers.

It was rumored that the mansion was haunted and that the people who lived inside were really ghosts of the original occupants. On several occasions people reported seeing cloudy specters weaving about inside. These apparitions always took place at night.

One night, when the sun was setting, the village children climbed the hill to the mansion. It was a windy day and the breath of the moldy house blew in their noses. It was initiation night. Stinky had to knock on the front door and howl "Boo!"

The gang shook hands with Stinky. Then Stinky, with a rock in hand, nervously walked up to the front door like a doomed man. He knocked gently at first, feeling the ping of the wooden door on his knuckles.

No reply.

The gang, hiding safely behind the scrawny shrubs. whispered loudly, "Knock harder."

He knocked until his knuckles were sore.

No reply.

So he banged the rock against the door, gouging the door in the process. Obtaining no reply, he pounded the rock harder and harder, louder and louder, until the house began to shake.

Suddenly the door swung open.

A horrible voice screamed, "Go away!"

No one noticed as Stinky and the gang panicked and scrambled home, but, peculiarly, the voice sounded just like Sparky, the leader of the gang.

Inversion Invasion

*T*he year is 2556 AD. We are in the midst of the Great War. The Nationalistics and the Independents can no longer coexist peacefully. A series of minor incidents, prodded by warmongers from both major factions, has finally plunged the Earth into a major war.

Somewhere in the middle of the battlefield is a loyal Nationalistics soldier. Her name is Colonel Sheree. She sits intently at her Utility Desk punching buttons on the consul. A dozen subordinates zigzag across the command center in a frenzy performing every order she gives.

"Two pips on channel six with brainwave pattern 0.58. Ten positions West," cries a Nationalistics subordinate.

"Set the neutralizer to frequency 1215!" shouts the Colonel in response. Then she mechanically punches a series of buttons on the consul and quickly squeezes the trigger. A burst of fiery red and white dots splash across the monitor.

"Good shot!" cries the subordinate.

Colonel Sheree does not smile. She shakes her head apprehensively and laments, "I'm afraid that shot may have given away out position. We reacted too fast."

A thundering flash blasts throughout the room, followed by an echo of screams. The Colonel looks down from her perch. Four of her subordinates are hit. They writhe on the floor.

"Everyone out before we are *inverted*!" she orders.

Too late. A second blinding flash, twice as powerful as the first, cascades through the room. Colonel Sheree and her subordinates are thrown to the floor. The pain is unbearable. Not physical pain but mental pain, like one super migraine headache that makes you bash your head into the ground.

Then suddenly the pain stops.

An eerie silence emanates across the air for a brief moment.

The Colonel jumps to her feet.

"Everybody up," she orders. "Back to your posts. We have a war to win."

Somewhere in the middle of the battlefield is a loyal Independents soldier. Her name is Colonel Sheree. She sits intently at her Utility Desk punching buttons on the consul. A dozen subordinates zigzag across the command center in a frenzy performing every order she gives.

Don't be a Pig

*N*ice red apple (cackle).
Looks (oink) delicious.
Want a bite (cackle)?
Looks (oink) juicy and sweet.
Go ahead. Take a bite (he, he, he).
No (oink) I . . . I . . . I better not.
See how red it is. See how it shines in the sunlight. I'm sure (cackle) it will melt in your mouth (he, he, he).
. . . But my mother told me never to take food from a witch (oink, oink).
Oh! Your mother is just an old fuddy duddy (cackle). Go on. Take a big bite.
. . . I . . . I . . . I don't know (oink).
You're hungry aren't you?
Sure (oink), I'm always hungry.
You don't want to starve? Do you?
. . . No . . .
(cackle) Then take a bite of the nice red apple.

But my mother said that witches can turn you into horrible animals (oink). I don't want to turn into a horrible animal.

Nonsense . . . Take a bite . . . It's sweet.

(oink) Sweet?

(cackle) Nice and sweet.

I like sweet apples (oink).

Well here. I brought this apple just for you because I know you like sweet apples (he, he, he).

. . . Well . . . Maybe . . . just . . . one . . . small . . . bite . . .

Yes (cackle), just one small bite.

. . . One . . . teeny . . . (oink) . . . weeny . . . bite . . .

Yes (cackle), just one teeny weeny bite.

Give me the apple (oink). (chomp) . . . Tastes (chomp) sweet (chomp) as (chomp, chomp) sugar . . . (chomp, chomp, chomp) . . . Real good (chomp, chomp) . . .

(cackle) (he, he, he).

Oh (oink) . . . Oh . . . I . . . feel . . . sick in the stomach . . . Oh.

(cackle) (he, he, he).

Oh . . . Look . . . (oink) . . . I'm changing . . . into a horrible animal . . . Oh . . . Help me . . . I'm changing into a horrible, grotesque, ugly human being . . . Oh . . . You witch . . .

Tester

*Y*es, I am the bubble-gum tester (phsst . . . pop). I am a professional tester hired to test the latest bubble-gum creations (chew . . . chew . . . phsst . . . pop). My experience spans forty-five years. Without my seal of approval, a new bubble-gum will not reach the market, for I am the connoisseur of bubble-gum.

Today I am going to test SUPER GUM, a new gum designed by multivariate computer analysis. Theoretically, this gum should outlast any gum on the market. Theoretically, it should have super elasticity with super pliability. Theoretically, it is the ideal bubble gum (chew . . . chew . . . phsst . . . pop).

A team of five dedicated scientists, equipped with the most modern computers and chemical knowledge, have devoted ten years of painstaking research to develop SUPER GUM. Finally the project has been completed. This new discovery will revolutionize the bubble-gum industry.

The hour of testing has finally arrived. The five scientists, the company president, vice president, secretarial staff, the plant managers and workers, and the press have all entered the ball field and have seated themselves around home plate, eager for the test to begin.

The band strikes up a resounding tune, loud and clear. A drum roll punctuates the excitement while I mechanically chew a large wad of SUPER GUM, softening it slowly for the big test.

What beautiful consistency. How easy it is to chew. How fast it softens in your mouth. And the flavor, a mixture of peppermint and licorice, is exquisite (chew . . . chew . . . chew . . .).

Time to blow the bubble. (phsst . . . phsst . . . phsst . . .). My, how big. And still growing. (phsst . . . phsst . . . phsst . . .). Bigger and bigger (phsst . . . phsst . . . phsst . . .) . . . Five foot diameter.

What's happening? My feet are lifting off the ground. (phsst . . . phsst . . . phsst). Still bigger. Ten foot diameter.

Bigger and bigger.

I'm floating in the air . . . Up . . . Up . . . Up . . . Into the clouds.

Help . . . Help . . . Help . . . How will I get down?

Up . . . Up . . . Up . . .

Higher and higher.

Faster and faster.

Help . . . Help . . . Help . . . How will I get down?

POP! Pffttt!

A Message from Grunnzas Snobzokas

TO: cOmmader gEneral frOm: grUnnzas sNobZokas

for nIgh onto seVen dAys i have oBserved frOm my sPace shIp, aLL the conFusion on the eArth beLow.

i have wAtched the eArthlings strUggle for liFe amOng themSelves. They feeD not onlY on the veGetation that flouRishes and nouRishes their weaK bOny bOdies, but they also feeD on otheR liVing sPecies as weLL.

tis a sicK, uGly and wickeD wOrld, i haVe obseRved. the eaRthlings, who doMinate this pLanet, are cruEl beYond beLief. they fiGht, cheaT, steAl and kiLL each oTHer.

undeR sePerate transMission i wiLL seNd piCtures of muRder, wAr and mAss deStrUction . . . of poWerful kiLLing weaPons . . . of torTure and dEAth . . . of a wOrld gOne inSane . . .

sUch a wOrld, if leT lOOse into ouTer sPace, wiLL surelY conTaminaTe aLL Other wOrlds. dOes not deServe to eXist in the uniVerse. the riSk is tOO grEat. ReCommend iMMediate comPlete aNNihilation of aLL liVing sPecies on eArth.

. . . traNsmission teMporarily inteRRupted . . .

as i seNd thIs meSSage i see soMe oBject moVing belOw. iT is a veRy tiNy oBject. mY cUriosity is aRoused and i mUst inVestigate.

pOwer cUt . . . mY sHip deSCends.

sUch aCtivity, i've neVer wiTnessed beFore.

i mUst go lOwer tO gEt a beTTer vieW.

pOwer cUt lOw. mY crAft deSCends.

mY mInd is fLabberGasted beYond all ken, fOr trUly i see a wOrld of peAce and haRmonY . . . of loVe and frieNdShip . . . of hArd wOrk and viGorous aCtivity . . . of prOgreSS . . .

pOwer cUt Off. mY shiP is laNded.

i reCline on the soiL, mY hEad neStled in mY Hands with elBows reSting in the saNd.

mY hEart is tOuched wIth the sCene i oBserve.

theSe sIx-leGGed cReatUres wOrk in hArmony. thEy mOve larGe sTones to diG their hoMes. thEy caRRy fOOd lOng disTances tO shAre wIth eaCh othEr. they shoW trUe lOve and aFFection . . . they rePresenT a perFect socieTY . . .

sUch cReatUres deServe eXistence. iniTial recoMMendation aBorted. the eArth mUst be sPared.

Living Ghosts

I do believe my house is haunted.

What makes you say that?

We hear footsteps in the attic. Chairs move about. Doors open and slam shut. At midnight the moaning starts. This has been going on since we moved into the house last week. My wife is a nervous wreck. She hasn't slept since . . . That is why I am seeking your professional help.

You've come to the right place, my dear chap. I am an expert on ghosts.

Tell me what I should do.

First you must understand that ghosts are real spirits. They eat and drink. They laugh and cry. Just like living beings. They have feelings. They are real just like you and me.

I do not understand.

They exist because they have excessively strong feelings, often brought on by a very emotional event, . . . an unsatisfied love affair, revenge for an unpunished crime, murder, or a need for forgiveness . . . Their emotions are so strong that even after death they still live. What you are experiencing is the excess, the spill over, from life. In time, these emotions will also die . . . But it will take a long time, depending on the degree of temperament . . . However, their demise can be accelerated by satisfying these persistent emotions.

How can I satisfy the emotions of a ghost?

If you encounter a ghost, you must speak to it with understanding. Do not be intimidated. Treat the ghost as you would treat any other living creature . . .

What do I do if it threatens me and my family?

Pray and bless yourself constantly. Use the Bible to protect yourself against a revengeful ghost who lashes out indiscriminately . . . But remember to offer your friendship . . . Find out what is troubling the restless spirit . . . Try to do it a favor . . . Remember that ghosts also live in the daytime as well as at night. They take many different forms.

How, then, can I tell who is and who is not a ghost.

Look into a mirror. A ghost has no mirror image . . .

I am beginning to understand what you mean. You have been a big help to me . . . Oh, my god!

What troubles you?

I am looking in that mirror . . . and I cannot see your reflection.

Do not be frightened. Please notice that you, too, have no reflection.

Sixth Dose

Tales Addicted

I write this message in desperation, with the hope that some specialist will read my story and offer me a cure.

My story begins a few years ago.

I accidentally found an unpublished manuscript buried among the books at the local library that I frequented. Each page of the manuscript contained a single, short tale. My curiosity got the better of me. So I sat down and began to read.

I was so fascinated by the first tale that I had to read the next one. The second story was more fascinating than the first.

The third was even more intriguing. Each story was more interesting than the previous stories. And before I knew what was happening, my mind was projected into new worlds, worlds beyond description.

My desire for these euphoric stories increased as I read each tale, a sensation I never experienced before. Time passed so quickly that I did not budge from my chair until the librarian tapped me on the shoulder to politely inform me that it was closing time.

Like a thief, I hid the manuscript under my coat and smuggled it through the doorway, undetected.

That night I did not sleep until I read all one hundred stories.

My nerves were on edge. My hands shook. My heart raced a mile a minute. My brain spun in dizzy circles. I was thirsty, thirsty for more tales.

So I did the only thing possible. I read the stories again, from page one to the very last page.

Unbelievable but true, so help me god, I found each story to be more intriguing than at first. This never happened to me before. Somehow, the underlying philosophy had escaped my attention during the first perusals. But now I began to appreciate the intrinsic meanings.

So I did the only thing possible. I read the stories again, from page one to the very last page.

This time I garnered a new perception. My eyes read between the lines. Words that were not on the printed page, popped into my head, filling the voids. The stories became a part of me and I became a part of the stories.

My urge to read these stories again and again has grown so intense that I cannot eat or sleep.

Heaven help me, I cannot stop.

World of Me

"*T*his world would be ideal if everyone were like me."

"That's not as impossible as it seems."

"I was only joking. No insults meant."

"But I am serious. What you said about living in a world full of yourself strikes me as a rather novel idea. Being an Anthropologist I find the idea rather intriguing . . . A social world where everyone has the same degree of instinct and intelligence . . . I know a professor of science who may be able to grant your wish . . . if you are willing to submit to a simple experiment."

"You have aroused my curiosity. Let us visit this professor."

. . . "You realize, genteelmen," the professor said, "thas thees leetle experiment weel not actually project you eento a world of *you*, but weel meerely reorganize your thinking patterns for zee interval thas you are under zee power of zee eloctronic brain."

"You mean like hypnosis?"

"Hypnosis only in zee eleementary sense of zee word. You see, zee thoughts thas are projected in zee mind weel be zee thoughts of your inner subconscious mind tuned by zee eloctronic brain. Your thoughts weel be focused on a world of *you*, only *you* and nobody else but *you*. The events will appear to be real although nothing external weel happen. Everytheeng weel be in zee mind."

"I do not understand, professor. But I am ready to visit the world of *me*. This should be exciting. Please proceed with the experiment."

"Very well. I place zee eloctronic brain over your head like thees. Set it for . . . ten meenutes . . . and throw zee switch . . . like thees."

"Professor, something is wrong. He is twitching and shaking. Turn it off!"

"No. No. Do not be alarmed. Thas eez simply zee aftershock. Nothing to be concerned about . . . See zee twitching has stopped . . . . Time eez up . . . Sweetch off . . ."

"Well, tell us, what was it like?"

"Professor, you must send me back!"

"Why? What happeened?"

"I'm not sure. Something strange has happened. I am not *me*. I am only one of *me*. The original *me* has gotten lost among the millions of *me*. I must go back. I must find my real self. I am lost."

"Good heavens, what have we done?"

Wiggle World of Colors

The blue lady shook her umbrella at little Billy Ooms. "Stop that laughing," she ordered. "Your mother should teach you some manners. It's not polite to laugh at people."

He stuck his tongue out as far as it could stretch. The insult took her breathe away. Billy watched the blue lady indignantly walk away. It was funny, the way she wiggled in contortions as she walked.

A green dog chased a green car. Billy giggled.

Then he saw a red man come out of the crooked house across the street. He disappeared as a blur. This world is so funny, he thought.

A yellowish couple, arm in arm, shivered in rhythmic patterns as they passed by. Billy chuckled. They looked at him sternly. He laughed louder.

What a crazy world, he mused.

An orange boy on a rubbery, orange bicycle bounced across the jagged road. He threw an orange paper into a zig-zag spin. It fell on the lopsided porch, which was also orange. This was so funny.

Billy laughed and laughed

A little purple girl stopped in front of him. When she moved, her face twisted into a thousand different shapes, some ugly and some funny. She looked at him. One ugly face stared at him. Billy moved his head from side to side and her face changed shape and her body twisted. He laughed real loud.

"What's so funny?" she asked scornfully.

"You are," he managed to say between his chortling. "You're all purple. Your face is like putty. You wiggle so funny when you move." His merriment grew louder.

"I am not purple, "the little girl said indignantly, "and I don't wiggle."

"Yes, you do," Billy shouted back.

"I do not."

Billy Ooms shook his head from side to side and watched her purple face twist, and melt, and grow, and shrink.

"How comical she looks," he said to himself

He laughed.

"My name is Patty Pots," she said. "Can I play your game?"

"Sure, here," replied Billy, handing her a crooked piece of colored glass.

Decision

Armed with a videocamera and a briefcase filled with notepads, paper and pens, Prof. Abraham Marcopolo smiled farewell, shook hands with his colleagues, and stepped into the time-flight chamber.

Ten years of grueling research were spent in developing the chamber. All preliminary tests gave positive indications that the chamber could navigate safely and accurately through time. Mice and monkeys served as test pilots during the initial development stages. Best of all, close examination showed absolutely no changes in physical and mental capacities upon their return from their time-flight missions. Unfortunately, the early pioneers were unable to convey, verbally, any of their experiences.

Marcopolo waved through the glass enclosure as he slowly faded away into the future.

The year was 1993. The time-flighter was set to project him two hundred years into the future. The plan was to observe and record everything possible within one year. And then to return to the present. He would bring back with him a glimpse of the future.

Who knows what wonderful things the future will bring?

A split second after disappearing from view, Prof. Marcopolo slowly began to reappear.

For a brief moment they all inhaled deeply and sighed

Most surprising and disappointing, the camera and briefcase did not return.

Something about the time traveler was different. He appeared to be younger, . . . stronger, . . . sharper . . .

"Tell us, doctor, what happened? . . . What was the future like? . . . Why did you return without any records?" A deluge of questions peppered his ears. His colleagues anxiously awaited his reply.

The puzzled time-traveler scratched his head and slowly replied, "I really don't know what happened . . ."

He paused, thinking, then added, "Deep down in my memory, I have an uneasy feeling that I had to make a decision . . . a decision to stay forever or to return without any record or recollection of where I had been, what I had seen, or what I experienced."

"And," he continued, "what puzzles me most of all, is . . . why I decided to return."

Beer Buddies

*B*uzz Barnaby had ordered his tenth bottle of beer when it happened. The bartender had ripped off the bottle cap with one swift jerk and pounded the bottle on the table in front of him, some beer foaming over the top and cascading down the side like soap bubbles.

Buzz had just poured himself a half glass of beer from the bottle when it happened. At first he didn't believe his ears. A bitter voice was calling from within the bottle.

"Dat blammed, why can't you be more careful," the voice said.

Then a tiny white-haired, white-bearded head popped up from the mouth of the bottle. Tiny fingers hung on tightly to the edge. "Dat blammed," the little man cursed and spat. Then his beady eyes caught sight of Buzz. "Well, don't stand there like an idiot," the little man said, "help me out."

He was three inches tall and as naked as a pig.

Buzz roared with laughter. Then with drunken dexterity swept him into his hat and quickly, but gently, folded the hat to imprison his precious, new friend. He laughed loud. Then downed the beer in one swoop.

"Hey, bartender! C'mere!" he called.

When the bartender approached, Buzz, with searching eyes, began to whisper, "I got something I want to show you. Should be worth a free beer."

As he listened, the bartender slovenly soaked up the spilled beer with a smelly rag and said, "What?"

Buzz surveyed the room. Then moved his hat forward.

"Nothin' doing," the bartender replied, "I don't buy hats."

"Not the hat," Buzz whispered irritatingly. "He's in the hat."

"Dat blammed," cried the little man in the hat.

The bartender was startled by the voice, jerked back and stared at the hat. "What was that?" he asked.

"Beer first," ordered Buzz.

The bartender couldn't hurry fast enough. He raced to the bar, grabbed another bottle of beer and the opener in one swift motion and then raced back to the table, flipping the cap on the way.

Buzz smiled as he grabbed the bottle and poured it into the glass.

"Dat blammed," cried a voice from the bottle in his hand.

"Dat blammed," cried a voice from the hat.

The Worst Battle

Sire, we are loosing the battle. Our men are on the verge of panic. Something must be done.

I know. I have fought many battles before, but this is the most dastardly battle of them all.

The enemy is relentless. Nothing seems to stop them. They strike day and night. There is no let up. Worst of all, they strike at night while we are sleeping. My men have not slept for two weeks and a day. They cannot continue.

This battle has me dumbfounded. There must be a solution.

How can we fight an enemy that we cannot see? They attack when we least expect.

Have you tried smoking the bastards out?

Yes, General Washington, bon fires are burning day and night. Mounds of billowing smoke from wet leaves permeate the entire area surrounding the camp grounds. Unfortunately, the fumes seem to choke us worse than the enemy.

What are our casualties?

Serious. Very serious. No man has been spared. Every man at Fort Nonsense and Jockey Hollow has been to the infirmary. The entire Continental Army is bleeding. The medics can't handle anymore.

This is the worst battle I have ever encountered.

The situation is most serious. Last night two of my best soldiers deserted their posts. They were fiercely attacked by an enemy they could not see. The bastards are invisible. They strike with venom.

How many of the bastards have you killed?

Thousands. But they keep coming. They must outnumber us by a thousand to one . . . More desertions are sure to follow. You must do something.

Order your men to keep well covered. Each soldier must protect himself as best as he can.

I have already done so. But it is so hot in this humid Summer air. The temperature has been hovering at 98 degrees for ten days, . . . the humidity has been close to 100%. A few more days of this torturous weather and a merciless enemy, and the battle will be lost. The men will desert for sure. Their nerves are on edge.

My nerves are on edge too. I have also felt the sting of the enemy. I have not been spared. Look at the welts on my hands and face. The battle with the Jersey mosquito has been the worst battle of my career.

The Winner

What happened to mayor Jacques Florino that night should not happen to a mangy dog on a rainy night. The mayor was invited to speak at the City Rotary Club. Election day was only a month away. This was a rare opportunity to campaign.

The unusually heavy rain and thunder that night caused local flooding. Unfortunately, the mayor's limousine got caught in a traffic jam and was delayed an hour. To make matters worse, in his haste into the hotel, he inadvertently left his prepared speech and spectacles in the limousine.

As he entered the side door to the stage, he was greeted with a friendly welcome and a dry towel. The program had already started. Several speakers completed their remarks. The master of ceremonies noticed the commotion off stage, smiled and said, ". . . And now we have one more important late contender to bring you an important message . . ."

The mayor strode onto the podium, chest out, shoulders square. He adjusted the microphone and stared into the fuzzy audience. He took a deep breath and said, "Ladies and gentlemen, good citizens, . . . I, mayor Jacques Florino, am greatly honored to be invited to speak to you on this important occasion . . .

"It has been a pleasure to serve as your mayor for the past four years. And with your support I hope to serve another four years.

"During my administration the crime rate has dropped twenty five percent, juvenile delinquency decreased fifty percent, all felons in the city government have been fired, nepotism has been eliminated . . . Honesty has been returned to the city government."

Cheers, clapping and whistling spewed from the audience, interrupting his speech. "How wonderful", the mayor mused.

He continued, "I have carefully examined the finances of the city . . . The budget is balanced. The city has ample money to meet all financial obligations. No further tax increase is necessary . . . In fact, if I am re-elected, I promise to lower taxes . . ."

The crowd raved wildly and rose to a standing ovation. When the hooting died down, the master of ceremonies shook the mayor's hand and handed him a trophy and a plaque. The mayor was puzzled. "Isn't this the Rotary Club meeting?" he asked.

"Hell, no," the host replied, "The Rotary Club is next door . . . This is the Liar's Club. You just won the top prize."

Jogging

Do you mind if I walk with you and ask you a few questions?

Be my guest.

Every morning, for the past few days, while I am jogging, I notice that our paths cross several times . . . However, you seem to be walking and diverting off the path . . . Do you take shortcuts?

No, of course not. I am exercising, just like you. But I do it in a different way.

Different? How different?

I used to jog. But not anymore . . . A year ago I suddenly realized that my whole life was on a fast pace. Everything was go, go, go. Then, one day, I read an article written by a medical expert who reported all the bad as well as the good features of jogging. Her conclusion was that walking achieved the same beneficial effects as jogging without incurring the bad effects.

Bad effects? What bad effects?

Overstimulating the heart. Foot injuries . . . caused by pounding the feet, with full weight, against hard macadam and concrete. Worst of all, spinal injuries. The spine is not designed to take such shock.

So you walk instead of run. And you take shortcuts to complete the circuit.

No, not exactly . . . There are other reasons.

Oh?

Philosophical reasons . . .

Oh?

Our world is too fast paced . . . Like Alice in Wonderland, I realized that I was running as fast as I could but still standing in one place. I was running so fast I did not see where I was going . . . Rushing about like a busy bee did not improve my quality of life . . . I was missing something . . . I was missing the most important things in life . . .

Oh? What important things?

We must take time to see, to explore, to enjoy the world around us . . . So, each morning I explore a different part of the park . . . This morning I diverted from the path and went through the cemetery . . . I read some of the engraved epitaphs and watched the birds land on the tombstones . . . I smelled the roses . . . I take a different path each morning, so each morning is a new adventure . . . Why don't you join me?

I wish I could . . . But I am much too busy. I must finish jogging before rushing to the office . . . I have a full schedule of meetings waiting for me . . . Sorry, but I must run ahead. Go, go, go, as they say.

Project Brain

$\mathcal{F}$or two years the worlds greatest scientist worked tirelessly on Project Brain. Project Brain was the most ambitious research project ever undertaken. It was designed to answer the most important question that has defied mankind.

Project Brain was the brainchild of Prof. Krupperman, a two-time Nobel laureate, recognized for his research into the Practical and Psychological Behavior of Computers.

Krupperman had convinced the world leaders to cooperate in assembling the world's biggest computer. This, he theorized, could be achieved by cross-linking every major computer in the world into a central computer, called The Brain, located in Melbourne, Australia.

Fiberglass cables were installed across every continent and the bottom of the seas. This took the best part of the first year. During the second year, each computer continuously feed data of every conceivable type into The Brain. This was done by scanning documents, encyclopedias, newspapers, movies, television programs and everything imaginable.

The Brain understood every language ever known to man. It had instant access to all information on earth. It knew every theoretical principle. It was infallible in grinding out the solution to any problem, . . . mathematical, social, political or scientific.

The final day had come. Reporters, cameramen, politicians and scientists gathered around The Brain, eager to learn the answer to the most baffling question.

The honor of questioning was given to Krupperman, who nervously stood on a small platform directly in front of The Brain. Dressed in his white laboratory coat, he held the microphone close to his mouth and spoke slowly and clearly. "Is there a God?" he asked.

The Brain flashed red and white lights, indicating that it was considering the question and searching for an answer.

One minute later, without warning, bolts of lightening shot forth from The Brain, striking various objects that burst into shreds. The building shook from the vibration. The thundering noise was deafening. Sparks flew every which way. The spectators, unharmed, were frightened beyond belief.

The Brain sent high currents of energy to each interfaced computer, burning each of them to a crisp.

Suddenly the awesome display of power stopped and the Brain spoke loudly, "Now there is!"

Extra Sensory Perception

*N*obody laughed when Sharon Holman, a self-proclaimed psychic, predicted that John Stotters would die today.

John Stotters was a scientist, recognized for his research into the paranormal. He used scientific methods, based on rigorous tests and statistics, to prove that no one on earth has ever had extra sensory perception. He wrote books on the subject and was the world's leading authority.

That afternoon Sharon Holman agreed to be tested by Stotters. The test was very simple. A deck of 52 playing cards was shuffled for ten minutes. Blindfolded and sitting backwards, the psychic was instructed to predict the value and the suite of each card before the card was turned face up from a face down pile. The test was conducted by none other than Dr. Stotters himself.

As the cards were turned over, each one matched perfectly with the predictions called out by Holman . . .

The agreement was uncanny. She foresaw all 52 cards without a single miscue.

In spite of this unbelievable score, Stotters still doubted her psychic ability. "You are a charlatan," he said. "The fact that you attained a perfect score proves that you are a fake.

"Dr. Stotters," implored the psychic, "how can you reach such a conclusion, when the evidence is so clear?"

"That's exactly the point," he responded sarcastically. "Your predictions follow statistical probability . . . According to statistics, for a deck of 52 cards, every *individual* arrangement is highly improbable. But, nevertheless, each shuffle of the deck *must* yield one of these highly improbable arrangements. Regardless of how improbable it may be, every arrangement is equally improbable . . . And that is what we have experienced here today . . . Your predictions were statistically probable. Nothing more or less . . ."

"But, Dr. Stotters, "How do you explain my feeling, my premonition, that you are going to die today?"

"Poppycock! I am as healthy as a horse."

"I have consented to one of your tests. Would you, in return, consent to one of my tests?"

"Fair enough. What is your test?"

"I place one bullet in the chamber of this gun . . . I spin the chamber like this . . . I put the gun to my head and pull the trigger like this . . . (click) . . . Now it is your turn, Dr. Stotters . . . Why do you hesitate?"

Seventh Dose

Variations on a Theme

John is an animal enthusiast who sleeps in the forest. Every day he talks to the animals. He loves animals. But the animals do not love him. One day they ate him. John does not feed the animals anymore . . .

Evelyn is a vegetarian who lives in the groves. Every day she waters and fertilizes the plants. She loves to eat fresh fruit and vegetables. But some of the vegetables do not always agree with her stomach. One day she ate some poisonous mushrooms. Evelyn does not eat vegetables anymore . . .

A million years ago, there was a hairy ape-man who lived among the dinosaurs. He was frightened by the dinosaurs. But the dinosaurs were not frightened by him. One day they accidentally stomped him into the ground. The ape-man will never be frightened again . . .

A thousand years ago, there existed a cave-man who lived by himself. He loved to eat animals. But the animals did not eat him. One day he met another animal just like himself. This animal tasted better than any other animal he had ever eaten . . .

A hundred years in the future, there will be a man who loves to breathe fresh air. But there will be little fresh air remaining. One day his breathing helmet will fail. And the polluted air will choke him to death . . .

A million years in the future, there will be a lonely man who pilots a spaceship. His destination will be to find people like himself somewhere out there in the universe. These people he will never find. Instead, his ship will turn into another meteorite in the heavens . . .

Today, there is a man who writes variations on a theme. He plays with words and philosophical concepts. He loves to create stories that shock the imaginations of his readers. But the stories do not always mean what he intended them to mean. Someday, these tales will return to haunt him. And he will be devoured by his own creative imaginations . . .

The Perfect
Food Processor

*T*his food processor will transform ordinary vegetables into a gourmets delight. It can be operated by any simple, ordinary, average individual, including jumble-fingered husbands who have no talent for cooking

Is there such a husband in the audience?

Yes, sir. Please step right up here.

I'll tell you what I want you to do. Take these carrots and drop them into the Perfect Food Processor . . . Add two eggs . . . Yes, crack them open first. Don't add the shells. Just the insides.

Fine.

Now add one lemon . . . Yes, the whole lemon with the rind.

Add a stick of butter, a dash of Worcestershire sauce, a sprinkle of sugar and, most importantly, a jigger of Kirschwasser and a jigger of Puerto Rican rum . . .

Fine.

Put the lid on and hold it down with your left hand.

Now turn on the Perfect Food Processor and watch the magic take place right in front of your very own eyes.

Fine.

Let's taste this culinary delight.

Hmm . . .

A little flat. Add another jigger of Kirschwasser and blend it with the processor.

Fine.

Let's taste.

Hmm. Not quite right . . .

Ah, yes. Of course, we must balance the Kirschwasser with rum. Add another jigger of rum and blend it for ten seconds . . .

Good.

Let's taste.

Hmm. Yesh, very good . . . Add a cup of rum . . .

Let's tashte.

Fantastic. The rum really helpsh. Add another cup of rum.

Lesh tashte.

Wowie . . . Absholu . . . tely shplendid.

Ha . . . ve anosher tashte. Thish ish absholutely the besht.

Now watch what happensh when I leave the lid off . . . and turn the Foo . . . ood Proshe . . . sher . . . on . . .

Wee! A magic . . . fountain . . . Ishn't that jush g r e a t?

Swamp Creature

*T*he little Irish village was settled next to the great swamp. During the daylight hours, the men of the village cut the bogs into bricks, stacked them for drying and later sold them as fuel. When the sun went down the villagers went home. No one ventured into the bogs at night because that was the time when the swamp creature appeared. Everyone believed in this folk tale, except Timothy McVee.

On several occasions when the workers were returning late and the sun was just beginning to set, Timothy would scare the living daylights out of them. He would hide behind one of the stone fences, and as they passed by, he would jump out, wave his hands high in the air and scream like a phantom.

After several frightful scares, one of the villagers challenged him, "If you are not afraid of the swamp, then go into the swamp one night and see what happens?"

"I do not believe in swamp devils," Timothy replied defiantly. "I will go tonight. I will take my lantern.

Nothing will happen to me. I will prove that there are no evil spirits in the swamp."

Some of the villagers wondered if they were wrong and Timothy was right. They decided to follow him secretly. They would stay far behind so he would be unaware of their presence.

The night was pitch black. The thick, low-lying clouds blocked out the moon. A thin misty fog blanketed the ground. It was relatively easy to follow Timothy because his lantern traced his path. Deeper and deeper they went into the swamp.

Suddenly, and unexpectedly, the wind blustered across their faces, chilling their skin and sending shivers through their bones. Another gust blew the lantern out. Timothy disappeared in the darkness. Everything went black.

Then, mysteriously, the clouds parted, allowing the moon to shine through. Outlined in front of them was the silhouette of a ghost, waving its arms and screaming damnations. They froze in their boots. And when the apparition moved closer and closer, screaming louder and louder, they bolted and ran back to the village, tripping along the way in the darkness.

The following morning, four delirious men described their frightening experience in the bogs. Timothy admitted that he saw the ghost. He swore, "I'll never again go into the swamp at night, so help me God!" Then he walked away with a devilish smile on his face.

Man of Destiny

As the mighty Caesar, I would conquer the horizon. With my trusty sword in hand, I would trample my enemies into dust, undo the plot of Brutus and slay the assassins. Empires would crumble under my feet. Cleopatra would be my slave. Pyramids would be built in my honor. My name would live forever . . .

. . . As Napoleon, I would create an invincible army. I would sink the British fleet, defeat Wellington at Waterloo, liberate France, vanquish the Grand Army of Russia, conquer the world. I would be a symbol of ultimate dictatorship, ruler of all kingdoms, a figure of strength, courage and power, feared yet envied and glorified. Josephine would sit at my side. Elba would be my castle. The Pope would crown me king . . .

. . . As Galileo, I would study mathematics and physics, and discover the secrets of nature. The astronomical riddles of the universe would yield to my inquisitions. But my research would go beyond the telescope. I would invent atomic reactors, build spaceships and conquer outer space. The Church would proclaim me a prophet and a saint. Religious zealots would honor me as their savior. The Earth would revolve around me. I would be the center of the universe. My brilliancy would be unparalleled throughout history, unequaled throughout eternity.

. . . As Houdini, no prison could hold me captive on Earth or in the heavens. My mastery of magic would be unsurpassed. The sun and moon would disappear on my command. At any instant I could become invisible or visible. With a whisk of my hand I could transform a man into a mouse and a mouse into a man. There would be no limit to my mystical powers . . .

. . . As Daniel Webster, my oratory would stir men to action, influence governments, move mountains, rock the world. My words would be impressive, dramatic, magnetic . . . I would rewrite history. My text would be revered like holy scripture. My words would live forever . . .

. . . As Rasputin, I would hypnotize the world. Everyone on earth would obey me. My mental powers would be irresistible. People would be my slaves. I would be God on earth . . .

"Adolph! Wake up! Stop daydreaming! How many times must I tell you to pay attention to class? You will never amount to anything."

Little Adolph Hitler lifted his head, looked up at his teacher, and grinned.

Here's to Heaven

$\mathcal{H}$e woke.

His ribs ached. The last thing he remembered was leaving the saloon. Dizzy from alcoholic euphoria, he lost his balance and stumbled into the street. From out of nowhere a gigantic truck came thundering at him, smashing him into the ground. He could still feel the wheels grinding across his ribs.

Joe Blansky rubbed his aching side, then looked around to see where he was. He expected to be in a hospital. But this was no hospital. He was seated in a wooden chair in front of a table.

He noticed all the liquor, an infinite supply. Racks of whiskey, of every conceivable variety, lined the walls from floor to ceiling. More than he could imagine drinking in a hundred lifetimes. His mouth watered and his eyes burned with anticipation. It was a dream come true.

On many occasions he proffered that "Heaven was an infinite supply of whiskey."

"Well, pour us a drink," said the man who sat at the other end of the table. Joe was startled. He had not noticed anyone else in the room before.

The stranger wore a black vested suit, white gloves, white silk shirt and a black bow tie. His hat and cane rested on the table. "Well, what do we drink?" he beckoned again

Joe Blansky smiled and said, "You're dead too. Aren't you?"

"Yes."

"Then this must be heaven," Sam remarked as he sprang out of the chair and jaunted to the nearest wall of liquor. He ceremoniously selected a bottle of Bavarian Rhine Rye, one of his favorites. The bottle was old and dusty. He unscrewed the cork nervously. Like a connoisseur he held the mouth of the bottle under his nose and inhaled the vapors. "Mm," he cooed. "The finest."

With steady hands he filled both whiskey glasses without spilling a drop. Then he lifted his glass, nodding to the stranger to take the other.

"Here's to Heaven," Joe toasted.

The stranger grinned and added, "Here's to Hell."

Joe swallowed his drink in one quick gulp. His mouth tightened, his eyebrows frowned. "This is nothing but water!" he cried while spitting on the floor.

The stranger smiled devilishly and said, "Hell, it is."

Who's There?

S top! Where do you think you are going?

Huh?

Where do you think you are going?

Who . . . who is speaking?

Me.

What? . . . Where? . . .

Over here . . . Turn around.

Huh?

Turn around?

I still can't see you . . .

Look up.

Where are you?

Just follow my instructions. Look to your right . . . No. No. The other way. Not to your left. To your right.

But . . . But . . .

No buts. Just do as I say. Turn to your right . . . and look up . . . Good . . . Very good . . . Now look up.

I still can't see you.

Don't look down . . . Look up . . . Raise your head and look up . . .

Take two small steps to the left.

Good.

I still can't see you. Who's there? Where are you?

Quiet!. Do as I say.

Where am I? What am I doing?

Be patient . . . Soon you will understand . . .

Understand what?

Please take four steps backwards. Be careful not to fall.

This is all so frustrating.

One more simple test and we will be finished.

Finished?

Bend your knees . . . up . . . and down . . . up . . . and down . . .

I still can't see you.

Hold still. Do not move. This adjustment is most critical.

Critical?

Just one little adjustment with the screwdriver in your neural nerve center . . . There . . . Now open your visual sensors . . .

I can see . . . But who are you?

I am your creator.

The Immortal
Doctor Horn

Do you believe in immortality?

No, Dr. Horn, frankly I do not. I know of no instance where this has been achieved. To develop a state of immortality requires altering our chemical, biological and physical structures . . .

But there is a very simple way to obtain immortality . . . More wine?

Yes, thank you . . . And, pray tell me, what is this simple way to obtain immortality?

We know that mental and muscular movements are controlled by electronic impulses. My theory, then, is simply that if these electronic impulses were replaced with permanent magnetic impulses, life would become permanent also.

Replace electric impulses with permanent magnetic impulses? Why, I never heard of such a ridiculous thing in my life.

It can be done.

Hogwash, Doctor, pure hogwash.

My experiments prove that I am correct.

Your theory is ridiculous. I would have to be insane to believe such nonsense.

But it's true. I've seen it with my own eyes.

Have you tried it on yourself?

Of course not. But I am seriously planning to experiment on human beings.

Doctor, I advise you to forget this idiotic idea . . . I'll have some more wine, thank you.

Would you like to witness a simple, little experiment that will make you change your mind?

I see no harm in it . . . I will be amused.

This wine we have been drinking has been subjected to specific dosages of beta and gamma radiation. Watch what happens when I spill a little of the wine on these straight pins . . .

Why, that's impossible. They're magnetized.

Permanently magnetized . . . And we have been drinking this wine all day.

Hogwash. I still don't believe you. This is some sort of trick.

Trick? Indeed . . . The wine has made us immortal . . . I'll show you conclusively . . . See? . . . This is no trick . . .

Doctor, what are you doing? Put down that knife, Doctor! What on earth are . . . agh!

Time to Go

$\mathcal{H}$e spiraled around her and exploded in a small puff of smoke. She coughed and turned madly around. "Why do you insist on doing these pranks?" she asked scornfully.

He reassembled himself and threw some sparks into the sky. "I'm happy," he replied.

She said crossly, "Be happy, but don't annoy."

"Well, the fact is, I feel it's time for me to go," he responded as he spun around in elliptical paths.

She vibrated nervously and asked, "Why must you go? Why is it that when we reach a certain age we must go?"

He looked at her annoyingly for asking such a basic question. After all, everyone leaves when it's time to go.

She contained herself and spoke tenderly. "Where are you going?"

"Oh, to the third planet from us. I think that's a lovely spot to touch down."

"This is all so confusing," she puzzled. "I don't understand."

"Don't understand what?"

"Why you are leaving."

"I don't really know myself. There is no reason. I just feel like I'm ready to leave . . . The energy inside me seems to be building up and I can hardly contain myself. Pretty soon a massive explosion will send me into outer space. My instincts tell me its almost time to go."

"But it must be a terrible feeling. Who knows what might be out there in space. Something could happen to you."

"Don't worry about such things. I used to think the same way. I never could understand why we must go. But, like I said, as the energy builds up inside, you know your time is nearly up."

"Please don't go."

"But I must. I can't explain it."

Three times he exploded in rapid succession. Each time he was able to reassemble himself. But the force inside was beginning to increase beyond containment. He directed his spiral, carefully aiming at the third planet.

Confused and crying, she watched him. He stopped long enough to say, "Goodbye," then exploded for the last time.

He shot out into the sky and headed, with the speed of light, as a packet of energy, to the third planet from the sun.

Never Say Die

*H*e was going to die.

The x-rays, electrocardiogram, magnetic resonance imaging, blood count and a myriad of other tests clearly indicated that he was going to die in three days, four hours and thirty seconds.

Dr. Longlife threw the charts on the floor, pounded his fists on the desk and filled his palms with tears. The one who least expected to die so soon, at age twenty-five, was going to die. He had already made many ingenious discoveries in medical science and had many more ideas to contribute. But his time was running out.

And he knew it.

There must be a solution. There must be some way to escape, some way to prolong his life.

With little sleep, food and water, Dr. Longlife concerted all of his efforts to solve this problem. And he had barely three days in which to so.

His observations were desperately keen. Matter and energy can neither be created nor destroyed, they can only be transformed into one another. Human thoughts are a form of energy and, therefore, cannot be destroyed. That means that thoughts can be transformed. But how?

Why are his thoughts confined to his frail, dying body? The body will surely die, but the mind can live. But how?

Dr. Longlife slapped his forehead and said to himself, "How stupid can I be? The solution is obvious. Transport the mind to a new location. Simple. So simple. Ever so simple . . . Thoughts are electrical impulses. Electrical impulses can be transported through metal conductors . . . That is the solution to everlasting life."

For three days he feverishly designed and built the thought-transformer. After the final wire was soldered in place, he lifted the electronic helmet high above his head and smiled. Only one minute of life remained. He had succeeded. His mind will not die.

He placed the helmet on his head, took a deep breath, and activated the transformer.

A blinding flash exploded. His screams pierced the air.

He found himself whizzing through space near the speed of light. There were a million tiny, high-pitched voices surrounding him. The world was blindingly brilliant. Sparks flew by him in all directions, like fireflies.

What a wonderful world, he thought, as he joined the other electrons that zipped by.

Food for Thought

Daddy, please tell me about the food people ate a hundred years ago. I am writing a report for English class and I thought that "food" would be an excellent theme.

Well, Sandra, many years ago food was quite different from what we eat today. Most food was cooked.

Cooked?

Yes, cooked in pots and pans on a stove. Especially meat.

People ate flesh?

Animals were raised to be eaten. They were killed, butchered, fried, dried, smoked, boiled or cooked, and eventually eaten as food.

How barbaric. I can't imagine people eating their pets. I get sick to the stomach just thinking about it.

Well, you must understand that a hundred years ago, protoplasmic food was not developed. The Genetic Age began when gene splicing was discovered in the later part of the twentieth century.

But why did they cook food? Why not eat it raw?

Food was cooked to enhance the flavor . . . and to kill germs.

Germs? What are germs?

Germs are microscopic organisms that carry disease. They feed on plants and animals. If they get inside your body they can make you mighty sick. In fact, some germs could actually kill a person.

How scary . . . Where are the germs today?

Germs still exist. But by genetic mutations they have been rendered harmless to the human body. In fact they are completely digestible. All diseases were eliminated during the Genetic Age.

What is disease?

Different types of germs would cause different maladies. Tuberculosis, for example, would create holes in the lungs, causing severe respiratory problems. Poliomyelitis would effect the motor sensors, causing paralysis and atrophy of the skeletal muscles, including the spine. People suffering from polio could not walk straight. Many had to use crutches or wheel chairs.

How gross . . . But getting back to plants and animals, did people really eat raw plants?

Indeed, they did. They ate apples, pears, oranges, picked fresh from trees.

And their stomachs could digest such barbaric garbage?

You must understand, Sandra, those were the days before the human body was transformed into perfection by gene splicing.

I'm glad I wasn't born in those days.

Eight Dose

The Monster Lives

Lying prone on the damp ground, the monster raised his head slowly, shook it from side to side to knock the dirt loose, and spat black saliva. It was not easy to walk at night. Freshly risen from a dead sleep, he had tripped over a loose stone and went sprawling into the muddy ditch.

The clouds parted, revealing a full moon that illuminated his ugly green skin, bloodshot bug eyes, pimply pickled nose, and a twisted mouth with mottled fangs protruding.

He snarled and coughed the dirt out of his mouth.

There was no doubt. This was the most ugly monster ever to inhabit the earth.

A gust of cold wind kicked up, throwing leaves and dirt into his face, smarting his eyes. He snarled and spat again.

This was his night to howl.

All living creatures were his prey.

He would show no mercy to whomever he met in the dark.

As he slowly rose from the ground a stray black cat spotted him from across the street. The cat stopped dead in its tracks, hunched its back, raised its hair on end, flicked its tail and hissed. The monster lunged forward growling and barking as the frightened cat scurried up the nearest tree to safety.

The monster, in torn rags, limped across the street, his hunched back waddling from side to side. It was not easy to walk in rotting clothes. The loose pieces would tangle his feet and cause him to stumble. But somehow he managed to drag forward without falling again.

He had already stalked two victims that eerie night and had sumptuously devoured their vitals. The taste was so invigorating that it sent his craving into high euphoria.

Now he fixed his attention on finding his next victim. Not a living soul could be seen. The street was deserted. But the lights were on at the house across the street. And that was were he was headed. To the house with the lights.

Slowly he climbed the steps.

The anticipation of his next meal made saliva drool from his mouth. His heart pounded with anxiety.

This was his night to feast.

He pressed the door bell and waited anxiously.

When the door opened, he screamed as loud as he could, "Trick or treat!"

This is My House

"*T*his is my houste."

"No, this is my house."

Fred Garble clenched his fist as his patience began to wear thin. "This is my house. So please get out of the way," he repeated.

Joe Murphy spat on the ground. His manner was no longer pleasant. "I don't know who you are. But this is my house. So kindly remove yourself from my property," he ordered.

Fred removed his handkerchief, wiped the perspiration from his forehead, pointed a finger at his adversary, and tried to talk calmly. "This is my property. If you don't get out of my way I will be forced to remove you physically."

Joe Murphy shook his head in disbelief. "Who do you think you are?" he shouted. "Get off my property."

"Your property. This is my property."

Both men looked to the sky in exasperation.

Neither moved a muscle. Inside, they burned.

"I have a key," exclaimed Fred, jangling his keys.

"So do I," answered Joe as he searched frantically through his trouser pockets, and triumphantly brandished his keys in the air.

In the meantime Fred inserted his key in the keyhole and flicked the lock open. "See!" he said. "My key fits perfectly."

Disgusted, Joe threw a punch aimed dead center for Fred's nose. But his hand passed right through as if his opponent were not there.

In reflex reaction, Fred tried to duck out of the way and at the same time he threw a counter punch to his opponent's midsection. His hand whizzed through causing him to fall to his own knees.

Puzzled, both men regained their footing, rushed at each other swinging their fists. But nothing happened. Their punches flew through the air as if neither were there.

They looked at each other quizzically.

Then they both dashed to the door of the house, bracing for the impending collision. When they reached the door, both of them blended into a single person.

Fred Barble stopped at the door, turned and looked around. "Where did the other fellow go?" he asked himself.

Joe Murphy stopped at the door, turned and looked around. "Where did the other fellow go?" he asked himself.

"What an odd experience," they thought.

Bracilli's Masterpiece

*F*inished at last.

Antonio Bracilli stepped backwards a few paces from the canvas, his eyes reveling in his painting. He inhaled deeply, relishing the aroma of the oils and turpentine. Then he slowly and gingerly let the aroma flow out from his lungs, as if he were giving the final blessing to his work.

It was truly a masterpiece.

Never in his seventy-two years of life had he achieved such success, such brilliance, such perfection. He was not only an artist but also a connoisseur of art. He knew he had, indeed, created a masterpiece.

The colors were vivid. Not too bright. Not too dark. Blended with superb preciseness . . . The trees were alive. The water seemed to flow with rhythm. The flowers were real. The sky had infinite depth. Lazy, white, cumulus clouds seemed to float in the air.

He knew he could never paint an equal. For an artist of his talent, this was a once-in-a-lifetime achievement. His talent was not inherited. On the contrary, he spent years of study, years of trial and error to reach this pinnacle. Nearing starvation, he had finally succeeded. His genius had finally emerged.

Tears of joy trickled down his face.

He had created a masterpiece far superior to the greatest paintings on earth. Undoubtedly, he will be famous throughout the world. How exhilarating were these thoughts.

The painting was sensual. It had a mystical quality. It teased the imagination. You could actually taste the dew on the grass, smell the flowers, feel the hot sunshine radiating from the picture . . . The leaves fluttered. The birds flapped their wings. The breeze blew across your face.

It was hypnotic.

It was bewitchingly real.

You felt that you could actually step into the picture.

Captivated by his own machination, that is exactly how Bracilli felt. It was exhilarating . . . And then he moved forward, lifted his left foot, and stepped into the painting . . .

In an attic in Greenwich Village there lives a lonely, forsaken artist. His name is Antonio Bracilli. He is an unrecognized artist. He claims to have painted the most brilliant masterpiece ever achieved . . . But no one believes him . . .

The Black Box

Before leaving, the doctor had given his assistant, Jebb, strict instructions *not* to open the black, wooden box under any circumstances. Jebb was puzzled. His curiosity gnawed at his nerves. The good doctor never gave such strict orders before. Why was he forbidden to open the box? What mysterious thing lies inside? These are the questions that bothered Jebb.

It was not the box itself that played on Jebb's mind, but the way in which the doctor so carefully emphasized the forbidding words. "Under *no* circumstances are you to open the black, wooden box," the doctor said, with heavy emphasis on the '*no.*'

"Understand?" The word 'Understand?' was stretched out with deliberate breath.

That was the situation.

The black box, six inches on each side, rested quietly on the desk, without a trace or a hint of what it contained. It did not move, nor make a sound. It sat silently.

Certainly, Jebb thought, if someone were to take a peek inside, no one would be the wiser. The doctor had left hours ago.

Then Jebb smiled widely and belched a whooping laugh. He had imagined that he had opened the box to see what was inside, . . . and guess what he saw? . . . The doctor . . . What a ridiculous sight . . . a tiny doctor, with a squeaky voice, chastising him for opening the box.

The smile disappeared and was replaced by fear. He suddenly imagined that the box contained a vampire bat. When he opened it, the bat flew out, flew over his head, circled over him several times and then bit him in the back of the neck, viciously. And he died on the spot.

But this is ridiculous, he thought. There is probably nothing in the box. It must be empty.

The doctor did not say anything about not touching the box, he reasoned. So, he picked it up and shook it quizzically.

Something bounced around inside. Something *was* inside.

He shook it again but it slipped from between his clumsy fingers and fell to the floor where the lid popped open.

By reflex, he jumped back.

His eyes filled with disbelief as the object inside scrambled to escape its prison. It flew out, flew over his head, circled over him several times and then bit him in the back of the neck, viciously.

Flying Saucers

*T*here are no flying saucers.

All those stories you have been reading in the newspapers are hogwash, pure hogwash, hogwash blown out of proportion.

It's a money making scheme.

Did you read about the chap in Colorado who said he saw a flying saucer land in the mountains? He climbed the mountain, saw the saucer, was greeted by green aliens, was invited inside, taken for a wild ride into the heavens at breakneck speed, and a year later released unharmed.

Guess what?

That chap is a millionaire today. He sold his story to the newspapers for a bundle of money. Then, to top it all, he wrote a best-seller book describing his adventures in the spaceship, and his visit to the outer space worlds.

Once the idea was planted in the minds of the public, mass hallucination inevitably sets in. Since then, thousands of sightings from all parts of the world have been reported.

To acerbate the situation, the government decided to investigate. They appointed a congressional committee who, in turn, appointed a fact finding committee who, in turn, appointed a team of scientists to investigate. Millions of dollars were appropriated for the investigation. And who do you think paid the bills? Yes sir. You and I and all the other honest tax payers.

Considering the time, effort and money spent, what did the committee find? Yes, sir, you guessed right. Not one shred of bona fide evidence.

The flying saucers turned out to be weather balloons, comets, kites, birds, planes, blimps, spotlights bouncing off low-lying clouds, and everything else imaginable.

Don't waste your hard-earned money nor your time reading all the nonsense printed about flying saucers.

There are no flying saucers. There never were. And there never will be.

Don't believe anything you haven't seen yourself.

Now, what in blazes is that whirling noise? And what in blazes is causing those flashing lights?

Oh, my god, it's landing right in front of me. A door is opening and a ramp is sliding out of the blasted thing. Little green men are marching down the ramp towards me.

Oh, my god, I don't believe it.

Vacation to
Outer Worlds

$\mathcal{A}$h, Smergley, I see you have returned from your trip to the Outer Worlds.

Yes, I took the last time lock from Megadon Center and just this very moment arrived home.

And how did you enjoy your vacation?

I traveled to many wonderful lands and saw many magnificent sights. It was a breath-taking adventure.

Did you enjoy the fifth dimension as much as you had expected?

Many times more than I had even dared to suppose. The speed at which the Transporter traveled completely reversed my life processes. Growing younger day by day was indeed a novel experience. Everyone should travel to the fifth dimension.

Ah, yes. But did you enjoy your trip into Subconscious Land?

At first it seemed frightening. But then I realized that it was only a world of dreams and was able to calm down . . . I must admit, however, that the horrible monsters that confronted me aged me a millennium, at least subconsciously.

What did you think of the Peggor Star?

Just another enormous mass of burning gases . . . Does not compare to the Romb Bomb.

And what did you think of Concerto World? I understand the place makes you feel euphoric.

Very euphoric. The perpetual sounds titillate your senses and emotions. The vibrations are delightful, like bathing in electricity.

What about the Psychic World?

Fantastic. Diverted. Schizophrenic. Most amusing. A delight of the first order.

Did you stop to visit Heaven World?

Yes.

And?

Quite dull. Uninteresting. Boring.

Of all the Worlds you visited which one stands out in your memory?

Without a doubt, Hell was most outlandish.

In what way?

Hell is a very different world. Very refreshing. Humorous. Sadistic. With huge red flames that dance spontaneously, accompanied by wailing, shrieking and screaming. The atmosphere curdles your blood. Emotions run high. It is unique.

Sounds so interesting. I think I'll go there on my next vacation.

Let's Eat

"**K**eep quiet, John. You're liable to get us both killed."

"Don't be silly. There's nobody around."

"Yes, but they might hear us, with you making all that confounded racket."

"Don't be so edgy."

"Sh! I think I hear someone coming."

"You're too tense, Mable. You keep hearing things that aren't there . . . Come now, let's enjoy ourselves."

"It's too dangerous," Mable whispered nervously, poking John to emphasize her words.

"Stop it! Stop it!" John screamed, pushing Mable away fiercely.

"Sh!" Mable was hearing things again.

"Shut up!" John's temper was rising. He began making louder noises, to spite Mable.

"As they entered the dining room, the aroma of a multitude of freshly cooked food captivated their olfactory senses. Spread out on the table was a feast of culinary delights.

"Look Mable, huckleberry pie, my favorite. Let's eat!"

John dug into the pie. "Mm . . . Delicious . . ."

Mable, overcome by the aroma, joined him in the feast. Within five minutes they surreptitiously gorged themselves, sampling bits of the different foods. Tasting each item. Licking their lips. Then tasting another and another. What a cornucopia of food, they thought to themselves. A feast fit for a king. How delightful.

The wine made them giddy. The more they drank the better it tasted.

Soon they were both singing loud and profundity, harmonious and discordant. Their euphoria was suddenly interrupted by sounds that emanated from the other room.

"John! John! I hear someone," Mable coughed out with her mouth full of food.

"Nonsense!" shouted John, louder than ever. Entranced deeply in wine stupor, he heard nothing.

Suddenly a strange man sneaked stealthily into the room, holding a weapon in his hand.

"I told you! I told you!" Mable screamed.

The man rushed toward them, raised his weapon and screamed with delight, "Pow! Pow! . . . Got them both." Then he walked away with his trusty flyswatter in hand.

Four Ace Bluff

Scarface stared at the cards in his hand . . . Four aces . . . Four beautiful aces . . . Four magnificent aces . . .

He didn't want to think about them . . . He didn't want to smile . . . He didn't want to frown . . . He needed his best poker face . . . No smile . . . No frown . . . No emotions . . . No sweat . . .

Four aces . . . Four wonderful aces . . . And Jimdandy didn't suspect a thing. He had skillfully slipped two aces from under the table which together with the two aces he was dealt made four beautiful aces.

The other three players had dropped out. But the money pot was big from the previous palavering.

Scarface acted cautious and thoughtful, stroking his beard. Then he raised the pot a thousand. Jimdandy smiled and raised the pot another thousand.

Scarface pushed his money into the pot. His palms itched. He was going to be rich. Every last dollar he had was riding on this hand.

But then he saw it.

His heart skipped a beat.

His throat went dry.

Two aces were hearts!

How could he have made such a blunder. If he showed his hand to Jimdandy, he could say goodbye to this world.

The room seemed to get hot. The perspiration on his neck started to steam.

No, this can't happen . . . Not now . . . Every dollar is riding on this hand . . . It's not so much the money . . . Life is sweet . . . and Jimdandy is the fastest gunman in the West . . . and the meanest.

"I call," Scarface choked.

"Four big kings," Jimdandy said, smearing the cards on the table.

"Beats me," Scarface scowled, throwing his cards helter skelter into the discard pile and then stomping out of the room, bitter and beaten . . . but alive.

Jimdandy, who was holding his breath all the while, let go with a huge bellowing sigh. Then he laughed until tears filled his eyes.

His hands swept in the money.

On the table lay four kings. No one noticed, two of them were clubs.

The Living Dead

Oliver Simms died on August 6, 1886. There was a funeral and he was buried the same day in a wooden coffin in the church cemetery . . . Nobody mourned his death, not even his family. He was a mean old bastard who beat his wife and children.

But six nights later he burrowed his way out of the coffin and came home. His wife and children were eating dinner when he walked in. Their faces turned ashen white from fright.

Oliver took off his dirty jacket, hung it on the hook, sat in his chair at the head of the table and growled, "I'm hungry . . . Pass the chicken . . . and the gravy . . ."

The family was too stupefied to move.

"What the devil is wrong?" Oliver snarled. "You all act like you've seen a damn ghost. Did someone die?"

"You did, last week," his widow replied nervously.

"Don't feel dead," he said. "Never felt better in my life."

"You don't look too good," his widow said, observing his skeleton face. "You're all skin and bones. You should go back to the grave where you belong."

"I'll go back when I feel dead . . . Pass the chicken. I'm starving. Haven't eaten in days."

"No!" widow Simms shouted. "It's a sin to feed the dead. No food for the dead."

As she went to grab the plate of chicken, Oliver seized her wrist with his bony fingers, pulled her hand to his mouth and chomped down hard. Her screams penetrated the air. Blood oozed out of Oliver's mouth as he chewed the meat.

The widow passed out and fell to the ground.

The children screamed and ran cowering away from the table.

Zeb, the oldest son, pulled a crucifix off the mantle, held it high in the air, casting a protective shadow across the face of his macabre father. "May God protect us from your evil spirit," Zeb cried.

But Oliver was not in the least deterred. He lunged at his son grabbing him by the throat, squeezing and wrenching his head from side to side, until Zeb became limp, dropped the crucifix, and fell to the floor . . . Oliver turned to face his other children . . . His smile was twisted and full of hate . . . "Who's next!"

A strange voice penetrated the silence. "Cut! Print it!" The director jumped from his chair and ran to congratulate the actors for a job, "Well done."

I am Going to
Kill You

You, out there.

This is your last warning.

I am going to kill you.

Yes, you. I mean you.

Don't try to run away. Don't try to hide. You cannot escape from me. No matter where you go, I will find you. There is no escaping me. There is no way out.

Run as fast as you can. Drive into the night without stopping.

Crawl under your bed. Hide in the closet.

Lock your doors. Bar the windows. There is no way to keep me out.

Buy a gun. Call the police. Be prepared.

When will I come?

Stand by the window. Wait for me, second by second, minute by minute, hour by hour, day by day. Your eyes will cry for mercy. Your hands will shake with fear. Your heart will pound like a jack hammer.

Am I in the closet? Am I under the bed?

Don't open that door. I may be on the other side.

I will lurk in every shadow. My eyes will follow every move you make. You cannot hide from me. I am everywhere, and yet I am nowhere to be seen.

But you will know that I am watching.

How will I kill you?

Ha! Ha! That's the best part. You won't know . . . until it happens. Then it will be too late to stop me.

Will I plunge a knife through your heart? Will I choke you with my bare hands? Will I shoot you in the back of your head?

I will not tell.

My secret is my pleasure.

Sleep no more. May your dreams be filled with nightmares.

Don't cry for help. No one will listen.

I am going to kill you, . . . and him, . . . and her. Nobody will be spared. Children, dogs, cats, . . . I am going to kill all of you.

And I am going to kill you to, doctor. When I get out of here, I am going to kill you first . . . And then I will kill everybody else . . . one by one . . . until no one is left.

. . . Soon, it will be your turn.

Ninth Dose

Let'a Me Alone

W̲ho'sa that come into the room? Who'sa that tryin'a catch me no lookin'? Think'a I no see?

All'a time they ruin'a my sleep. Look'a them. Tryin'a make me come. Scratchin' on'a the floor.

kitchy coo . . . kitchy coo . . .

Look'a that. Make'a noises again. All'a time bother me. What'sa matter these people. Go get'a my milk, instead'a make with the nonsense.

pss . . . pss . . . pss . . .

Oh, mama mia. Go away and let'a me rest in'a peace and quiet. Why you make'a me jump'a for nothing? You wan' something? Go do it you'self. Don'ta pest'a me.

meow . . . meow . . .

For heaven's sake. If that'sa the cat talk, I'ma the pig. I make'a the better sound when I'ma sick. Go away. Don'ta bother me. Can't you see I'ma da sleep.

here pussy . . . here pussy . . .

I no wan' come. I'ma da sleep.

here pussy . . .

You make'a me mad. You wan' me come? I come. I come and give'a you a big'a bite, an' scratch'a yo' hand. That'sa what I do. Go 'way.

shoo . . . shoo . . . shoo . . .

Oh. You make'a me real mad now. I scratch'a you good. Don'ta kick'a me. You cause'a more trouble.

out . . . out . . .

What'sa matter you. All'a time make'a da noises. Don'ta you speak English? I can'ta understand a word'a yo' say.

out . . . out . . .

Alright. I go down'a da cellar. Just stop'a da push.

out . . . out . . .

Don'ta push. I go. I go.

out . . . out . . .

Stop'a da push. I go down'a cellar.

Maybe now I get'a some rest. The rats don'ta bother so much.

Earth Shaker

*O*ne cannot describe in words the excitement felt by Nikola Tesla on the 3rd of July 1899. He was anxious to test his new theory. That night, the moment of truth was at hand.

He theorized that the Earth was a huge container filled with electrical fluid. By vibrating the Earth this fluid could be set in motion, causing standing waves. Such resonance would transfer vast amounts of energy from one point on the Earth to another.

A mile east of Colorado Springs, Tesla built an experimental station. It resembled a ship with an eighty-foot tower, moored on a prairie. A copper ball, three feet in diameter, rested on the top of a metal mast that extended 122 feet in the air above the tower.

Inside the station, high-frequency transformers of various shapes and sizes were neatly connected into the primary circuit, ready to drive the magnifying transmitter.

For the event, Tesla wore his black Prince Albert coat, gloves and a black derby hat. Only he and his faithful cohort, Czito, would witness this most important experiment in the history of mankind. The building was safely fenced off and warnings "KEEP OUT—GREAT DANGER" were prominently posted.

Tesla ordered Czito to throw the master switch on. The effects were spectacular. Fire and lightning crackled across the secondary coil. Tesla gleamed with excitement.

Electrical sparks exploded in all directions filling the air with the stench of ozone. Snakes of flame writhed across the coils. Lightning bolts shot out of the copper ball striking the ground again and again in every direction. The Earth began to vibrate.

Cattle stampeded. The thunder and vibrations were felt fifteen miles away. People thought it was the end of the world.

Tesla gloated. Soon, he surmised, the other side of the Earth would vibrate with equal ferociousness. This experiment would prove how a small amount of energy could be magnified a billion fold and transported across the Earth.

Then suddenly everything went deafeningly silent. The power went off. The electric power plant in Colorado Springs burst into flame and the city fell into darkness. The experiment was over.

We may never know if Tesla was correct. Who would dare repeat the experiment?

Visit Our World

*T*his is a strange world.

A strange world, indeed!

Just think . . . We exist as long as you read our story . . .
And we die as soon as you stop reading . . .

A strange world, indeed!

We have no mortal bodies, yet we exist. Without your
help we cannot live, because the place where we live is in
your mind.

When you stop reading, we stop living.

If you are a slow reader, so much the better, for we
shall exist so much longer. But if you are a speed reader,
we shall live for only a brief moment. So, please read
slowly.

We can bring you joy and happiness, or sadness. But
we have little choice in this matter. Our positions in life
are determined solely by our Creator, the Author.

By reading, you bring us to life.

It feels good to flow through your mind, to mingle
with the thousands of complex thoughts that find refuge
there.

We treasure life as much as any animate creature. But we can only live as long as you continue to read. When you stop, our life stops. We become petrified, reduced to dormant words on a printed page.

Would you venture to say that we live in another dimension? Perhaps, the fourth dimension? A dimension that has neither length nor width nor depth. But existence. The dimension of thought . . .

Pray tell, we have untold power . . . We can influence your opinion . . . The pen is mightier than the sword . . . Thoughts are more important than deeds . . . From thoughts come deeds . . . Thoughts are the seeds of deeds . . .

Surely, you must enjoy our symbiotic relationship. As long as you continue to read these words, we will share our thoughts with you. The rest of the world, temporarily, seizes to exist. Our partnership is truly amicable. You must agree, it is a unique, exquisite and enlightening experience.

If you should tire, let someone else read this page. We can exist in a host of different minds.

Do not abandon us.

We love your company.

Come visit our world again.

Siesta Dreams

"Don't dream during siesta time," cautioned Carmina.

"Why not?" asked Ricardo, her visiting cousin.

"Because, in Dry Valley, siesta dreams come true."

"Nonsense."

"Oh, si, they do come true. I'll prove it . . . Let us go and speak to tio Pedro."

She grabbed Ricardo by the sleeve and pulled him across the street to Pedro who was taking a siesta in the shade of the porch of his grocery store. She shook Pedro on the shoulder and startled him awake. "Tell Ricardo about how siesta dreams come true in Dry Valley, tio Pedro."

"Oh, si," he said with a sleepy tongue. "Siesta dreams come true in Dry Valley . . . The other day I dreamt my burro she run away, and the next day she run away . . . Then I dream my barn she burn down, and the next day she burn down . . . Si, siesta dreams come true. One must dream only good dreams during siesta."

"See, Ricardo, I told you."

"Well, you are too late," Ricardo said. "I already dreamt."

"I hope it was a good dream," Pedro cautioned.

"I dreamt some bandits on horses robbed your store."

"Oh, mama mio!" cried Pedro.

"And they shot and killed you."

"When did you have this dream?"

"Yesterday."

"Oh, mama mio! Where is my gun? I must protect myself. Oh, mama Mio! I am doomed."

Pedro ran into the store as he saw, in the distance, four men on horses galloping towards his store.

But they did not stop at the store. They did not carry guns. They rode past without hesitation. They seemed to be in a hurry to get to wherever they were going.

"See, my dream did not come true," Ricardo chastised. "They did not rob and shoot tio Pedro. How do you explain that?"

"I also had a dream," answered Carmina. "I dreamt that four men on horses galloped through town without stopping."

Just then a cloud of dust kicked up over the horizon. In the far distance one could observe four men on horses approaching.

They carried guns.

Everybody's Food

*T*he mono-wheeled egg mobile whizzed through the cities at supersonic speed. It carried the ambassador of Fowlovia to the Intergalactic Union Conference . . . He was several minutes late.

It screeched to an abrupt stop at the capitol steps. The ambassador, a two legged, dizzy-looking bird with a long neck and a small head, with glasses perched precariously on the tip of his beak, dashed awkwardly up the steps.

On his way into the Chamber he heard the representative of the Solar System shouting protestations in echoing tones, ". . . such actions are utterly abhorrent. I, therefore, propose that all Galaxies refrain from eating any form of human beings, whether or not they are intelligent or dumb in comparison to the prominent species living on that Galaxy . . ."

The Fowlovian ambassador strutted majestically across the floor shouting, "I am entirely sympathetic to the views expressed by the ambassador from the Solar System. Cannibalistic actions against Fowlovians and their related species must also stop. I propose that all forms of bird eggs remain under Intergalactic Protection. I propose that no eggs or bird creatures be consumed by any species in the Galaxy . . ."

Just then a dozen ambassadors from Herbia pushed their way into the auditorium. The tall, orange-colored ambassador spoke loudest, "We are in sympathy with the Fowlovian and Solarian ambassadors. Similar circumstances exist with regard to Herbians . . . We propose that all vegetable life be allowed to live in peace and tranquility, and not be subjected to the devouring action of other species . . . Some members of the Herbian family are rooted to the ground and are unable to protect themselves. It is disheartening to see . . ."

Then another voice boomed above the rest. The ambassador from Liquidos slid into the room, hardly able to contain himself as a gelatinous form on this strange world. He cried loudly as he poured across the aisle toward the podium, "I protest the misuse and slavery of lower forms of Liquidos. I propose an act of emancipation to free all liquid life in the Universe . . . All forms of liquid must be allowed to leave their prison worlds and migrate to Liquidos, where they will be given sanctuary . . ."

All the delegates protested and bickered at the Conference. It ended with the ambassadors eating each other . . . Thus began the War of the Universe.

Out of Body Experience

*H*ow do you know there is no life on Mars?

I have been there.

How are you able to do that without leaving the Earth?

Yesterday, I had an out of body experience.

Please explain.

Last night I had a deep sleep. My inner self escaped from my body. I slowly floated upwards out of my body into the air . . . As I looked down, I could see myself sleeping soundly . . . By waving my arms I could propel myself in any direction . . . as smooth as a feather drifting in the atmosphere . . .

Yes. Yes. Then what happened?

For some unknown reason I began to move my arms like a bird moves its wings. As I moved them faster and faster, I rose higher and higher into the sky . . . And before I realized what was happening, I found myself whizzing through outer space faster than the speed of light . . . It was breathtaking . . . The stars sparkled as bright as beacons . . . It was dazzling . . .

But what about Mars?

Finally, after what seemed like a euphoric bath in the heavens, I found myself circling a planet . . . The planet was Mars . . . As my arms tired, I slowly began to descend from the heavens to the surface of Mars . . .

Mars? How did you know it was Mars?

I just knew it was Mars. Something inside my head told me it was Mars. I really don't know how I knew. I just knew . . . Why do you ask such a dumb question?

So? What was Mars like?

Like a red desert . . .

There was nothing there . . . absolutely nothing . . . There were no trees, no grass, no plants . . . no water . . . There were no animals, no bugs, no ants, . . . no people . . . nothing but red sand and red stone . . . Everything was red . . . Even the sky was red . . .

So? What did you do there?

I explored everything I could find . . . every rock . . . every rock formation . . . every sand dune . . . every hill . . . every valley . . .

That must have taken you a long time to do?

Not at all. By flapping my arms I could fly anywhere I wanted. And I did just that . . . I zipped across the entire planet in no time at all . . .

And now your back to Earth.

Not quite . . . My inner self is still on Mars, and does not want to return. My outer self is here on Earth . . . You see, I am only half here.

Your Time is Up

*T*he telephone rang.

Gladys lifted the receiver, said, "Hello?" and then slammed the receiver down.

"Who was it?" asked Roseanne.

"Oh, just a wrong number again," Gladys lied, trying not to frighten her roommate. She turned back to her textbooks, trying to gain enough composure to concentrate on studying for tomorrow's chemistry examination.

"That's the third wrong number this evening," Roseanne said.

The phone rang again. But this time Roseanne picked up the receiver. "Hello?" she said sweetly.

The voice on the phone was raspy and diabolical. *"Your time is up. At ten o'clock tonight I am going to shock you."*

"Is this some kind of joke?" she asked. But the voice hung up.

Gladys shook her head and spoke. "Pay no attention . . . Some prankster is having fun tonight."

"Sick humor, if you ask me," Roseanne added. "Did you hear what that jerk said? . . . He said he was going to *shock* me . . ."

"Yeah, that's what he said to me too."

The phone rang again.

"Don't answer it," shouted Gladys, but Roseanne had already lifted the receiver and before she could say anything the malicious voice said, "*Your time is up. At ten o'clock tonight I am going to shock you.*"

"Stop harassing . . . You're sick," Roseanne said with a strong sense of irritation flooding her body.

They tried to resume their studies but the ugly voice kept ringing through their minds.

At precisely ten o'clock the phone rang again, setting their nerves on edge. Without noticing the time Roseanne grabbed the phone, and screamed painfully as her hand became magnetically glued to the receiver. Seeing her roommate in pain, Gladys quickly wrenched the chord out of the wall disconnecting the phone, experiencing an electric shock in the process. The pain stopped, and Roseanne dropped the phone.

Shivering and crying, Roseanne sat back. "It tried to electrocute me," she said.

"Well, it's disconnected. So there is nothing to worry about now," Roseanne added.

Then the phone rang and an ugly voice said, "*Your time is up.*"

We Come in Peath

I am Bleen.
I am Gleen.
Gleen ith my younger brother.
Bleen ith my older brother.
I am ten yearth old and my brother is thix.
We come in peath.
We come from outer thpace. We traveled many yearth to reach your planet. Our trip wath plotted carefully by integrated charth and today, by intergalactic tranthportation, we have arrived thafely.
Why do you giggle?
We have thudied your language carefully. That ith why we are able to thpeak to you tho clearly.
Why do you laugh?
We want to be your friend. We mean you no harm. We come in peath. Take uth to your leader.
We tell the truth.
We come in peath.
Do not laugh. Your laughter ith inthulting.

It ith important for uth to agree on peath as thoon ath pothible . . . Do not laugh . . . Your laughter ith inthulting. If you continue to laugh we will be forthed to eliminate you.

Thop laughing or I will fire my ray gun!

Thupid idiot.

Bzzt. Bzzt. POW!

Thupid idiot . . . We come to make peath and he laughth at uth. No wonder there ith no peath on Earth. Everyone laughth at peath. That ith the fifteenth Earthling we have had to eliminate today. Thupid idioth are not fit to live. How can we negotiate peath when no one will lithen?

We will juth have to make them lithen. We muth make the Univerthe thafe from future war. It ith our duty. That ith why we were thent here.

Yeth. Your are right brother Gleen.

We muth not give up hope. We muth keep trying.

Look. Over there . . . There ith another Earthling on the bridge, fishing in the pond.

Yes. Yes. Let uth approach him.

We come in peath.

The Perfect
Chicken

*N*ow that is impressive. I've never seen anything like it . . . a silver chicken. Is it alive?

No, it's a mechanical chicken . . . a robot . . . I call her Henrietta.

That's even more impressive. A mechanical robot that looks like a chicken, walks like a chicken, sounds like a chicken, and eats like a chicken.

Yes, it is my attempt to create the perfect chicken.

Except for the metallic sheen, I would believe it to be alive. How do real chickens react to Henrietta?

The hens had no problem accepting Henrietta as one of their own. But all the roosters in the pen have chipped beaks, strained necks and broken claws . . . They learned very quickly not to attempt to proliferate with Henrietta, much to their disconcertation.

Why is she going into the empty coop?

By my watch, it is time for her to lay an egg.

The robot lays eggs?

Yes, she lays an egg every hour, twenty four hours per day.

That's twenty four eggs per day. That is remarkable.

What is more impressive is the shape of the egg. Take a look at the egg she just laid.

My god, it's a cube.

Same size as an ordinary egg, but cubical. It will not roll off a table, and its shape makes it ideal for packaging.

But its silvery.

The metallic shell is much stronger than an ordinary egg. See how it bounces on the floor and does not break.

Remarkable . . . But then, how do you break open the egg?

With this special vise I designed . . . By turning the screw, the egg center will crack open with no problem . . . no splinters . . . no chips . . . just a nice clean split to release the contents, like this. See?

I'm impressed.

You can cook the egg sunny-side up or scrambled. The egg can be soft boiled or hard boiled, same as a real egg.

Very Impressive. You've created the perfect chicken that lays the perfect egg.

Not quite. There are a few bugs that have to be worked out.

Oh?

Here, taste this egg that I just cooked.

Ugh! Metallic.

See what I mean?

Such Useless Thing

*M*agor, quick, come see what I have found.

Foolish Nabzot, now what did you do?

I have found something strange. Nothing I ever have seen the likes of before. It scared me half to death.

Silly Nabzot, what is it that you find?

I know not. But it is very strange . . . It moves . . .

If it moves, it must be alive. I shall ask it if it lives . . . Most unusual thing, do you live?

It does not answer.

Can it be that it does not live . . . yet moves?

I do not understand this. It moved most peculiar down the hill. It came towards me with rapid speed, stopped only by the bushes.

It is flat . . . How can it move?

It is very strange indeed.

Perhaps it is magic?

Do not be superstitious, Magor. It is of this earth. I will make it move by scaring it . . . Shoo! . . . Shoo! . . . Boo! . . . Boo! . . .

It does not move.

Maybe I should poke it with this stick . . . There . . . There . . . Move . . . Move . . .

It does not move.

It moved before . . . It is flat and but it is also round . . . When it moved it stood upright . . . like this . . . See . . . like this . . .

Yes, I see how you lift it upright . . . But it does not move . . . It falls over flat when you let go.

I will lift it again and roll it over to the edge . . . Help me . . .

It is heavy.

Push! Push! Push it to the edge of the cliff . . . Now, one more push . . . and over the edge it goes . . . Look! . . . It moves down the hill with rapid speed! . . . It goes wheeeee!

Such a useless thing, Nabzot . . . Do not waste your time with such useless things.

Look how it bounces . . . twists . . . and falls flat . . . Fascinating . . .

Useless, utterly useless . . . Let us go.

I must give this thing a name . . . I shall call it . . . wheel.

That is a worthy name for such a useless thing . . . Now come, let us leave it to itself.

You are right, Magor. It is useless. Let us return to our cave.

Tenth Dose

Freeing the English

*H*alt! Who goes there?

It is I, Webster.

Why are you here?

I have been sent on a mission to free the English.

Balderdash! I know of no such mission . . . Where are your papers?

I need no papers . . . You dare not stop me from doing my duty . . . I am here to free the English and I intend to start this very minute . . .

Begone! I cannot let you through without permission!

For too long the people have been enslaved by the poor English. It is time to convert the English so that everyone can live a happier and a simpler life. The English is too difficult to tolerate. People must be free to speak and to write as they wish . . . I have a most important task to perform . . .

I cannot let you pass.

You must let me pass . . . I created the problem many years ago . . . I am responsible for the misery suffered by millions of people . . . I am the one who enslaved the people . . . I am the one who wrote the rules and the laws . . . I am the one who set the unbearable standards . . .

Get away from here. I will not listen to the rambling of a madman.

I am not a madman. I have risen from the grave. My soul has suffered too long and too much for the abominable damage that I have done, for the misery that I have caused. I have come here to correct my mistakes. I cannot rest until I have completed my task . . . I have come to convert the English . . .

Begone! You cannot enter here.

A curse will be placed on your soul if you do not let me pass . . .

Saints alive . . . I am being threatened by a ghost . . . Dare I defy a spirit from the netherworld?

Let me through before I am forced to pass an evil spell on your spirit that will condemn you to the fires of Hell for eternity!

Pass! . . . But do your duty quickly and begone forever . . .

I, Webster frum the grayv, heerbi decree that the English iz free! Furthermor, frum this da forth, I further dekree that al men r free tu spel English wurds az they so deezir . . . Al dikshunarees r heerbi abolishd . . . Al wurdz r heerbi emansipated . . . Reed and ryt az u so pleez . . . Al ruls of spelyng r disolved . . . The English iz free . . . Ma god bles this da . . .

Ur tym iz up! Pleez leev! Mai ur spirit forevr rest in pees . . .

The Secret to a
Long Life

*T*oday, great Guru, we honor you on your one hundred and fifteen birthday. What is the secret to your long life?

The secret to a longer and a better life is through meditation . . . Meditation is an ancient practice, known to bring spiritual benefits, relief from daily stress of daily life, and improvement in health.

Teach me to meditate.

Yes, my son. Sit here, next to me. Fold your legs like this, like a pretzel, and sit perfectly still.

Like this?

Yes. Now close your eyes and close your mind. Make your mind blank, completely blank. You must see nothing but darkness. Not a single thought must enter your mind.

Hmm . . . That is not easy to do.

When thoughtlessness is achieved the mind enters the spiritual world. A serene numbness envelopes the entire body. The euphoria is beyond measurement and description.

It is a hypnotic state that elevates the inner soul to heavenly peace, replenishing the psychic underpinnings of the brain and the body . . .

Hmm . . . For a brief second, I did make my mind blank.

Meditation requires much concentration . . . and much practice . . . When achieved, all stress vanishes. It is a relaxing therapy. Nothing matters because, in the meditating state, there is nothing to cause anxiety . . .

Hmm . . . Yes, you are right . . . When my mind went blank for a brief moment, I did feel a spiritual serenity, . . . a calming sensation, . . . a warmth, . . . an inner peace . . . But I could only blank out my thoughts for a fleeting moment.

Do not expect success immediately. As you gain strength your ability to make your mind thoughtless will increase. Eventually you will be able to meditate for several minutes. With practice your meditation will increase to hours at a time, several times a day.

Oh, great Guru, as an accomplished practitioner, how often and how long do you meditate?

I meditate three times a day, for six hours at each stretch.

That is remarkable . . . That means you meditate eighteen hours each day . . . What do you do in between?

Eat and sleep, of course. Deep meditation is not easy to achieve. It requires controlled concentration which is very, very tiring.

Oh, great Guru, you have enlightened me. I will practice until I can reach your exalted level . . . I look forward to a very long life.

The Guillotine

"*H*ow, in Heaven's name, did I get into this predicament?" Suzan Kaplan asked herself. There she was, her head and hands locked firmly and securely in the stock . . . helpless . . . captive . . . on public display for everyone to see her inevitable execution.

This was not the eighteenth century. This was the nineteenth century, 1893. The world was civilized.

There was no trial. She committed no crime. She was selected at random, a victim of statistics. Anyone else could just as easily have been chosen. Why her?

Her heart pounded fiercely. Her mind wandered randomly from one memory to another, and then back to reality. She was locked in a guillotine. There was no way out.

Before imprisoning her in the device, the executioner had sharpened the blade, oiled the pulley and tested the mechanism several times. He would pull the blade to the extreme top and then release it. The blade thundered with diabolical force as it came smashing to the base.

This he repeated several agonizing times, until Suzan turned pale and felt dizzy from fright.

How could this be happening? She was not a witch. She was only eighteen years old. She was too young to die.

Silence overcame the crowd as the executioner waved his hands and slowly raised the blade.

Suzan, head firmly secured in position, closed her eyes as tight as humanly possible. The last thing she heard was the rumbling of the blade as it wrecked down upon her.

Her head fell into the basket. The blade, smeared with blood, glistened in the opening. Suzan's body draped limply, lifelessly.

The crowd was mortified into dead silence.

After a brief moment, the executioner reached down and lifted Suzan's head from the basket. With blood dripping, he flipped it several times in the air, spinning it like a basketball.

Several people screamed and fainted.

Then he knelt in front of the guillotine, placed the decapitated head onto the blade in the opening. He held it there with one hand while the other hand pulled the rope, lifting the blade upward. Then he flipped the lock mechanism open.

Suzan stood upright, sighed with relief, smiled, and walked off the stage as the Great Maldini, magician extraordinary, bowed gracefully to the thunderous applause that followed.

Defender of the Universe

*I*NTRUDER ALERT! . . . INTRUDER ALERT! . . .

The message flashed across the terminal screen. Panic whistles screamed at full blast.

A bright white, blinking blip on the screen clearly showed the position of the intruder. It was headed straight for the center of the Armada.

The adrenalin was pumping through the Commanders system. "I've got to stop it!" he screamed. "I've got to stop it before it reaches the perimeter or the Armada will be destroyed."

But how? The intruder had already penetrated the outer defense system. It was firing deadly missiles in all directions with excruciating accuracy. The defense satellites were exploding one after the other. Their signals on the screen disappeared, one by the other, in rapid succession. The intruder was a Level 100 Jetfighter, the fastest and most accurate.

The Commander, palms sweating, pressed Defense Code 2 button. The screen flashed, "INSUFFICIENT MANPOWER . . . DEFENSE ORDER ABORTED . . ."

The Commander jumped up nervously . . . punching different Defense Codes, one after the other. Each time the screen flashed, "INSUFFICIENT MANPOWER . . . DEFENSE ORDER ABORTED . . ."

On the verge of panic, he punched the GIVE STATUS button. The computer responded, "Energy shield penetrated. Security squadron eliminated. Intruder now entering inner level at full strength in Zone 3, Epicenter 5.

Nervously the Commander aimed at Zone 3 and Epicenter 5 and squeezed the trigger sending a burst of twenty missiles that scattered like buckshot in all directions toward the bandit intruder. The intruder dodged right and left. One missile glazed the bandit, damaging it, . . . but did not stop it.

It fired back at the middle of the Armada.

The panic sirens blared louder and louder as the Armada ships were being destroyed, one by one, with deadly accuracy.

"Fire at will," ordered the Commander in desperation.

Tracer bullets flashed across the screen as the surviving Armada ships fired at the intruder, aimlessly. Puffs of explosions filled the screen like fireworks.

"We've lost the battle," cried the Commander as a message flashed across the video terminal: GAME OVER . . . Please insert 50 cents to continue . . .

Vengeance is Mine

*T*he sky was dark, except for the full moon. A dusty mist had settled in the valley making the night unusually cold and damp.

It was a night not fit for man or beast.

Near the pond, south of the village, at the end of the river of Moss, there lies a body buried secretly in the soft earth, murdered by none other than Bull Rainey, foreman of the Town Mine. There lies Jack Jacobs, murdered for ten thousand dollars, his life savings from laboring in the mine for sixty-one years.

From the village tavern, the voices of hearty laughter echoed through the valley. Above all could be heard the deep ugly laughter of Bull Rainey, enough to raise the dead.

As midnight passed, the sounds in the tavern eventually disappeared, except for the brazen booming voice of Bull Rainey. Not until Bull was thoroughly saturated with vintage was the innkeeper able to close his doors.

Bull lived across town.

And to get across town he had to pass near the pond, south of the village, at the end of the river of Moss, where lies a body secretly buried in the soft earth.

Only Bull knew the exact spot where Jack Jacob was buried. It was two paces southwest of the great dead elm. Bull carved the initials JJ into the dead tree, a fitting marker for a dead man.

In a humorous mood, he decided to pay his respects to the dead man. So he took a minute detour to visit the grave of his unwitting benefactor.

Through the foggy mist he kicked aside the the leaves and spat on the secret grave.

A sudden ear-splitting scream resonated in the valley, as a bony hand pushed up through the earth, grabbed Bull firmly by the leg, and pulled him into the soil. His leg slowly sunk into the soft, muddy earth.

A voice beneath the ground growled with hate, "Vengeance is mine."

The death grip was like a vise of steel.

Bull was no coward.

He pulled his switch-blade knife from his pocket. There was but one thing to do and he did it.

To this day no one knows how Bull Rainey got his peg leg . . . But we do . . . It was down near the pond, south of the village, at the end of the river of Moss

The Thought Transcriptor

$\mathcal{H}$ow could you have done such a thing, Cardwell?

I don't know. It's just one of those things that start out with good intentions, but somehow gets out of hand and before you realize what has happened it's too late.

Why did you build it?

It was an obsession that grew into reality . . . I wanted to build a machine that would record everyone's thoughts and words, creating a permanent record of every conceived concept.

That's exactly what's wrong. Every word, every thought is captured by the Thought Transcriptor. There are no private thoughts. We live in constant fear of revealing our innermost secrets. There is no moment of peace.

I know. I know.

Even our dreams are recorded. I'm afraid to sleep anymore. In fact, this very conversation is being recorded . . . Cardwell, you have created a monster . . .

You have robbed us of our privacy . . . Do you realize what is happening?

Only too well, Baizely.

The State Police have taken complete control of the Thought Transcriptor. They use it to track down political enemies as well as criminals. The slightest infraction, the slightest thought, the slightest disagreement with the State is detectable . . . People are being sent to prison for simply thinking against the State, even for the briefest moment.

It is unfortunate that the Transcriptor is being used for such a dastardly purpose.

It must be destroyed . . . But it is indestructible . . . We are doomed. Worst of all, this very conversation will send us to prison. The words we speak are testimony of our guilt.

Do not panic. There is a solution.

How can an indestructible machine be destroyed?

It can't.

Then, what solution is possible? I do not understand.

There is a simple answer . . . Erase the thought before it reaches the Transcriptor.

How is that possible?

With this Thought Eradicator I have just finished building . . . By pressing this button, every thought in the world will be erased . . .

You are a genius, Cardwell. You are smarter than yourself.

Peacemaker

Wherefore art thou going?

To bring peace to this dastardly world.

Who giveth thee charge to perform such a task?

I have been summoned by the Lord Almighty, himself. Last night he appeareth before me in my dreams and ordereth me to purify this sinful world. He is pained by the evil that groweth so strong. There are too many sinners.

And how, pray tell, arth thou going to bring peace to this wicked and sinful world?

We must eliminate the evil doers. Evil begets evil. One small venial sin, in time, inevitably leads to mortal sin.

True. But how dost thou rid evil?

Step by step. I am to carry out the first step in God's plan.

And what is the first step?

There are too many murderers. There is too much killing. God detests killing. I detest killing. That is why the Lord has chosen me to fulfill his command. We must make the world a safe place to live. We must bring peace and tranquility.

But how dost thou bring peace and tranquility?

By eliminating all killers.

And how dost thou eliminate killers?

By slaying them. By slaying every one of them, we will eliminate the killers. When there are no more killers the world will be a safe place to live. There will be no fear of being murdered.

But, sire, if you slay the killers, wouldst not that act, in itself, make thee a killer too. Wouldst not, then, thou be equally guilty of murder?

Yes, thou speaketh the truth. Slaying the killers would condemn me to Hell . . . But I have been orderth by the Almighty, and I dare not disobey him.

If thou slay all killers then thou will become a killer.

Yes, but I must obey God. I have no choice.

Then thou must obey God to the fullest.

Yes, to the fullest.

That leaves thee no choice in the end.

Indeed. In the end, after slaying all the sinful killers, I have no choice but to rid this world of the very last killer.

Who wouldst that be, sire?

Need you ask?

The Gourmet

Our guest this evening is Julio Burpp, the world-famous, gourmet cook and distinguished author of seventeen cook books . . . Let's have a round of applause for our guest . . .

Clap! Clap! Clap!

Please be seated Mr. Burpp . . .

Your latest book, that I hold up to the television camera for everyone to see, contains over 1500 recipes . . . Are these all original?

Yes, they're all perfectly original. Created by me alone.

That's an awful lot of original recipes . . . Are the recipes in your other sixteen cook books also original?

Yes, every one is original.

Each book contains over one thousand recipes. In fact, I counted a total of over 21,500 recipes . . . That's a lot of original recipes . . . Are there any duplicate recipes in these books?

No sir. Every single recipe is unique. No two recipes are alike.

Have you actually cooked and tasted all 21,500 recipes?

No . . . That's impossible. I don't have the time, nor the patience to cook and sample that many dishes.

If you don't taste your own culinary creations, how can you be sure they are good?

I have a trained palette. My taste buds can sense the ingredients as I compose a recipe. As I create each recipe, my mouth salivates, producing the exact flavors called for. These flavors become enhanced, in my mind, as I add the cooking instructions.

Well, that is a most amazing talent. You are truly gifted . . .

I was born with a gift of taste. Over the years I have nurtured that gift to perfection.

You truly are amazing, Mr. Burpp . . .

We plan to put you to the test . . . While we were talking, Mr. Chavez DeLaroy, the head chef at the Vanderocker Hotel, has been busy cooking two gourmet dishes. Only one of them is taken from your latest book . . . Please taste each dish and tell us which one is yours . . .

Mmm . . . This one is terrible. Bitter. Acid. Foul-smelling . . .

And the other?

Mmm . . . This one is delicious. Aromatic. Sweet. Smooth.

Most interesting, Mr. Burpp . . . The first one is from your book . . . And the second one is made from dog biscuits and cat chow soaked in vinegar and beer overnight.

Psychophilic

I don't know why I was sent here. I'm perfectly healthy. I feel fine. Nothing bothers me.

This is just a routine check-up. Sometimes there are hidden internal problems which, in later life, catch up with you when it's too late to do anything about it. You wouldn't want that to happen to you, would you, Mr. Webb?

This is ridiculous. Why are you strapping me in?

These aren't straps. They're recording sensors that send your emotional stress signals into the computer for analysis . . . Now please relax while I make the necessary adjustments . . . The expansion tube goes across your chest, like this . . . The heart magnometer goes right here . . . And the biodopter fits over your head, just so . . . Fine . . . We're all set . . . Switch on . . .

Oh, that tickles.

Reaction profile 654. Excellent. Passion flux 453. Good.

Doc, what do all those dials mean?

They record your reactivity to the different impulses.

Are my impulses good?

Very interesting. Let me finish my measurements. Then I'll tell you what I have found . . . Exopuric susceptibility 946. Glandular spurt 678 . . .

Finished . . . Now for the final confirmation by the chart . . .

Chart?

The chart is the summary report compiled by the computer. In a few seconds all of your data will be processed, and a final diagnosis will be printed on the output card . . . Ah, here it is now,

What does it say?

Just as I thought.

Is it good or bad?

You're Psychophilic. I'll have to operate immediately.

Operate? Psychophilic? What's going on? Let me loose.

Psychophilics attract psychologically unstable inebriates. It is very serious. I must operate immediately.

What's that buzzing sound? What are you doing to my leg? Aeeiouu!

Bone structure is good. I'll send this down to the lab for further analysis . . . Dr. Scrumpf, come in here. I've got one of those rare Psychophilic cases we've been waiting for for years. Perhaps you can finish your experiments with Streptocillin Choli on a live one.

No, Not Again

No, not again.
I cannot do it.

I've done it many times before, but I cannot do it anymore. I must rest and relax. Over stimulation may be fatal.

No, not again.
I must rest.

A body can only take so much punishment. It is inhuman to ask me to continue . . . particularly when health and sanity are at high risk.

No, not again.
I will not do it.

To attempt to create one more masterpiece, at this time, will undoubtedly result in permanent insomnia, irreversible paranoia, dual schizophrenia and severe prosopagnosia.

No, not again.
I refuse to do it.

I know you are looking forward to another ingenious creation, but I am exhausted. My creative efforts have drained every ounce of energy from my body and soul. My brain needs time to recharge. I must rest before I blow a mental fuse.

I can barely keep my eyelids open. My eyes roll in dizzy circles. The room is spinning. Numbness penetrates my hands and feet. I can no longer stand. Every bone in my frail body aches with excruciating pain. My condition has reached a critical stage.

I am too weak.
My mind is a blank.
I cannot go on.

I implore you. I beg you. Please don't ask me to tell you another abstract tale.